GET YOUR COCK OUT

A romance by
Mark Manning

ATTACK! is an imprint of Creation books

First published in 2000 by ATTACK! Books
www.creationbooks.com
Copyright: Mark Manning 2000 AD
Design by Rom
Original artwork by Paul McAffery
Printed and bound in Great Britain by
Woolnough Bookbinding Ltd
Irthlingborough, Northants

The right of Mark Manning to be identified as the author of this work has been asserted by him in accordance with the Copyright, Designs and Patents Acts of 1998.

All rights reserved. And that means ALL rights, motherfucker! No part of this publication may be reproduced, stored in a retrieval system, or transmitted in any form or by any means, electronic, mechanical, photocopying, or otherwise, without the prior permission of both the copyright owner and the above publisher of this book.

WARNING: This book is probably the most disgusting you have ever read. No, we're not joking, we mean REALLY disgusting. Readers of a weaselly, prissy and humourless disposition should put this book down now and choose something by that nice Will Self instead. Look, when we say "disgusting" we're not messing about. We've cut loads of stuff out of the original manuscript but what's left is so sordid it unfailingly has us puking our guts up in disgust every time we read it.
 And we're hard.

Also published by ATTACK! books

Satan! Satan! Satan! by Tony White
Raiders Of The Low Forehead by Stanley Manly
Tits-Out Teenage Terror Totty by Steven Wells
Whips, Furs and Leather by Jesus H. Christ
Vatican Bloodbath by Tommy Udo

and coming soon....

Bloody Heroes by Bob Morris
Tokyo Blodbath 2002 by Stanley Manly
Ebola 3000 by Dick Marshall

All *ATTACK!* books can be ordered for £6.99 each from
www.creationbooks.com
or
Creation Books 4th Floor, City House,
72-80 Leather Lane London EC1N 7TR

GET YOUR COCK OUT

is sincerely dedicated to:

**Cobalt Stargazer, Kid Chaos, Slam
Thunderhide, Tex Diablo, Evil Bastard,
Robbie Vom, Flash Bastard,
Trash D. Garbage, Bill Drummond
and, of course, Gimpo.**

Fuck it, go on then, and Dave 'fucking' Balfe.

Chapter One

Get Your Cock Out

Mincey Harris, lead vocalist with The Leather Cowboys, pushed his copy of Anal Madonna under his mattress and wiped his bell-end on the crusty duvet.

Pushing his long black hair out of his eyes he lit his first reefer of the day.

Mincey and his band had a support gig that night with a bunch of talentless assholes called The Tramps Of Dawn.

Mincey had a bad feeling about this. Musically he knew his band would blow the Tramps completely off stage, but there was...something....

Mince raised a cheek and let fly a blurter. Miraculously he needed a shit.

Mincey had been rocking for nearly twenty years and it showed. His skeletal physique had more to do with poverty than the drugs, but they didn't help.

He boiled up his morning shot and dug the spike into his eye. It was the only place left he could still get the shit into his body.

The smack was no longer pleasurable, hadn't been for years. It just got him out of bed in the same way other people used caffeine.

He took the first shit he'd had for over a month. The single black pellet splashed in the filthy water. Mince hung on hopefully. That must have been the donut he ate last Thursday.

He picked up a magazine from the dirty linoleum. The face of Peter Darklord, the haunted front man of the Tramps, stared back at him trying to look spooky and mysterious.

Although Mince knew in his soul that his band the Cowboys were Gods of Rock, he knew deep down that the Tramps were the real thing too.

So did a lot of other people.

The gig tonight was a secret warm-up for the Tramps who were playing at Wembley Stadium the following night.

This Darklord guy, like Mincey himself, had it, (whatever it was).

But the Mincer's senses also told him that this guy also had that. Mincey didn't know what that was either - and for some instinctive reason he didn't want to find out.

The Tramps had specifically asked for The Cowboys as a support down at The Shit And Shovel, a truly horrible rock club in Soho.

Mincey's antennae were shaking paranoid. Why?

Why did the Tramps specifically want the Cowboys on the bill?

Mincey had made it clear in the press promotion for their last CD, 'Get Your Cock Out', that he was no big Tramps fan.

There was something funny about the whole thing. But the bread they were receiving for the two gigs was far too much to ignore, it could even be the break they'd been searching for over the past 20 years.

Chapter Two

Rock God Nad Jam

Peter Darklord lay back on his bed sipping a glass of absinthe. The fiery fin de siecle poison felt good burning in his stomach. Tara Emerson Lake Dogshit-Ffuck-ffeatures coughed as the Mysterious Rock God blobbed-off on her tonsils without the slightest twitch or muscle spasm. One minute she's fellating the dark star, the next moment she's almost drowning on the two pints of Rock God nad-jam pulsing down her windpipe.

She tried to pull her head away but the effete singer, showing a strength that defied his svelte appearance, pulled her face even further onto his bloodhammer, almost choking her.

He eventually released his grip and her ladyship pulled away coughing and wiping the mess from her face. It tasted horrible.

Tara, like most aristocratic females was something of a connoisseur of sperm, able to tell with stunning accuracy what the lucky spunker's diet had consisted of over the previous two days.

There was something...something deliciously wrong about Darklord, his sperm tasted of blood - blood and ice cream. If it were made by Ben and Jerry it would have been called Clotted Cream, clotted as in blood clots. It was sweet yet it had the unmistakable coppery tint of fresh plasma.

She fingered the silver crucifix around her neck.

Surely not! she thought.

"Why that's ridiculous!" she muttered to herself as she skipped to the bathroom to wash her gash. The cool water soothed her bruised cunt. Darklord lacked nothing in the leather trousers department and how he had managed to get that purple monster up her barking spider was anyone's guess.

"Vampire!" she laughed stepping into the shower. Peter must have quite literally fucked her stupid! Nanny had always said that her imagination would run away with with her one day. He'd obviously been eating a very rare steak or something.

Stupid girl!

Chapter Three

Space Age Boogie

"All that facking goth crap as well, man!" said Mincey to his reflection in the dirty bathroom mirror. The brown had straightened him out, he felt almost chipper.

"Stupid facker!" he laughed, pulling on his leather strides. Everyone knew all that vampire/undead shit was well past its sell-by date.

The thing was, though, Darklord and the Tramps were raking in the cash by the truckload. The American market being at least 20 years behind the UK, the sons of Uncle Sam in the malls and wastelands of the Midwest were lapping this shit up like vampires partying hearty in a bloodbank

Mincey threw on the Cowboys' latest CD. He still thought that Strutter's guitar was way too high in the mix, you could hardly hear Mincey's vocals on some of the tracks. He turned up the volume as 'Blow Job Queen' snarled out of his speakers.

Mincey started strutting in front of the mirror, doing his rooster-walk, hands on hips, head jutting backwards and forwards.

He sang along.

"Blow job queen, you know what I mean, she's outrageous, oh yeah!"

'BJ Queen', as it was known to the fans, didn't even make the Top 100 but that didn't surprise the Mincer, every one knew the charts were rigged by the Cosmosodomistic Black Gas Corporation pushing their evil subliminals, brainwashing the masses, making them bow down to the dollar God.

"Well fuck the dollar God!" said the Mincer.

The kids dug The Leather Cowboys and their spaced-out brand of space age boogie and that was what was important. Yeah.

Mince applied his black eye liner and admired his pout.

No way did he look 45, under the lights he could pass for an 18 year old easily. That was the smack, it made you look younger, everyone knew that. Mince slammed the door and rocked down the street, leaning forward like he was just about to fall over, avoiding people's eyes. That was why no one ever recognised him. Eye contact, man, just focus on your own energy. Don't let the squares drag you down.

"Yeah man, rocking!" he mumbled to himself.

Chapter Four

Dandelion Dandelion

Dandelion Dandelion was shedding slash with excitement. Tonight at the Shit and Shovel two of her most fantastic super-hero Rock God bands in the world ever - The Tramps of Dawn and The Leather Cowboys - were playing a secret gig.

The Tramps wanted to play at the venue they first started up at as a warm-up for Wembley .

Her father - he was dead now, passed away last year - had been a massive fan of The Cowboys. She'd been reared on their music, the Cowboys were the soundtrack to her life. 'Turd Burglar', released in the '70s, was the album her mother and father were listening to when Dandy was conceived.

When Dad died last year they played his favourite Cowboys' song at the funeral. 'Salami Sam And The Slider' - a beautiful acoustic number that could still make Dandy cry. Dad looked so beautiful in his coffin, dressed in his leathers, favourite purple ruffled silk shirt and real Texan cowboy boots. The guy at the funeral parlour had done them proud, Dad's make-up looked great.

Although Mincey and the boys would always hold a special place in her heart, there was something frighteningly attractive about Peter Darklord, the singer with The Tramps of Dawn. He used to play lead drums with Gormenghast, the '70s prog rock band before forming the Tramps in the mid-'80's.

He was frightening and sexy at the same time.

She'd fantasised about him dressed in his black robes taking her off to his castle in the wild mountains of Bingley in West Yorkshire and ravishing her bumhole through her knickers more than once. She blushed at the memory.

But it was Mincey who held the key to her heart, she felt a real connection to the 45 year old singer of The Leather Cowboys even though she'd never met him.

Dandelion was no groupie. Sometimes though, when the Cowboys were rocking down at the Colepitz on Kilburn High Road, she'd wished she was.

Mincey recognises her of course, she goes to every gig the Cowboys play, sometimes she's sure all those saucy winks and erotic tongue flickering are aimed just at her.

"Oh Mincey!" she sighed, collapsing onto her bed, clutching the ticket for tonight's gig against her firm yet ample 16 year old breasts.

Dandelion didn't have many friends her own age, in fact she didn't have any friends at all. They were so stupid, into all those stupid indie bands with their tinny guitars and squeaky voices.

Although Mincey probably weighed less than 7 stone, he was all-man.

His voice dripped experience.

Dandelion put on the Cowboys new CD 'Blow Job Queen' and sang along with the chorus.

"Blow job queen, you know what I mean, she's outrageous, oh yeah!" .

Strutter Sandinista, the gorgeous bone-thin lead guitarist, scorched out of the speakers with one of his fantastic solos. When Strutter rocked it was as if the heavens and all of hell had collided, his pyrotechnical digital-wizardry defied description. She could see them now rocking the house down at 'Wank de L'amour ' - the last glam rock club in town.

Gerry Enchilada, the beefy Mexican bass player, rock-solid behind his skinny mirror shades.

Robierre Le Vomiteur, the cool Gitane smoking drummer, knocking the shit out of his kit bollock-naked, his big old French dick swinging along to that crazy beat. Actually Robierre was from Leicester, he'd played with the hip sixties band Crazyhead but somehow, in only the way rock'n'roll permitted, he'd convinced himself he was from the slums of Paris and that he used to play skins for the Velvet Underground.

Dandelion couldn't understand why The Leather Cowboys weren't the No.1 band in the world, people were so stupid, couldn't they see? Were they blind or something?

Chapter Five

Crispin St Albans

The Shit and Shovel was rammed. It was supposed to be a secret gig. Yeah, sure!

The place could hold about 400 punters on a good night, there was more than twice that many tonight. Press from right across the board - from the fashionable sTyLe magazines to the neanderthal metal rags - they were all there to see the first British band to really slay the Yanks since the days of Led Zep, Black Sabbath, Free, Yes and, of course, The Deep Purples.

Darklord's band The Tramps Of Dawn played a strange mixture of Black Sabbath type riffs funked up and screwed around with all kinds of complicated breakbeats and sampled weirdness, Darklord himself fucking around with a huge phalanx of antique analog moog synthesizers and weird shit he'd made himself out of old shortwave radios.

"Tapping into the music of the spheres" is how he described it in one of his rare interviews.

Steven Wells from the influential music weekly NME had been quoted as saying that Darklord was probably the only musician of the past 20 years that could possibly be accused of being a genuine genius. From anyone else this would have just been more hyperbole, but from Wells it was taken straight. The Northern skinhead knew his shit from his shinola. It had been over 20 years since the bad tempered writer had said anything positive about anyone apart from obscure Nordic Black Metal bands that many people thought were figments of the eccentric writer's imagination.

It has to be said that on certain occasions the avant garde screams emanating from Darklord's arsenal of synths -

cranked out at deafening volumes, combined with the pulsating boom of the bass drum and the hard rocking antique metal riffs - could take you completely out of your mind. 'Transcendental Tower Of Dreams', the second CD from the Tramps, was a classic by anyone's standards. The music Darklord had been making with Gormenghast seemed to have come alive with his new band.

It's no secret that Darklord and Gormenghast's original front man, the blonde pretty boy from Kent, Crispin St Albans, had hated each other with a passion. God knows how much bad water, heartbreak and lawyer's fees had sailed under that notorious bridge of sour litigation in the late '70s.

Darklord was accused by many old Gormenghast fans of driving the sensitive St Albans to an early grave. He was found dead in the bath of his small Parisian apartment in Montmarte in '82. The case, a suspected homicide, was still open.

Chapter Six

Cosmic Turkey

Mincey and the boys laid into the mean rider with disdain.

"The fackin beer's not even cold!" spat Strutter, tossing the can of cheap rats' piss at the heavily graffitied wall.

"Got any gear Mince, come on, man, just a line..."

Mincey begrudgingly chopped out as small a line of brown as he thought he could get away with. Apart from Strutter, who dabbled, the rest of the band - Robierre and Enchilado - could take or leave hard drugs.

Alcohol at arse-splitting quantities was more their bag - the truth being that they were lazy bastards. Why bother waiting for the man when you could achieve oblivion with a couple of bottles of vodka at a fraction of the price from any high street in the country?

"You would have thought those bastard facking Tramps of Facking Dawn or whatever they're facking called would have facking laid something on for us! Look at this, man, these facking peanuts, they're not even facking KP!" moaned Strutter, backcombing his black hair into a bouffanted vulture's nest and gassing it with half a can of industrial-strength hair spray.

"Fackers!" he grunted, straightening his bollocks in the skin tight leathers and pushing his spam this way and that to achieve the desired effect.

There was a knock on the door.

"Tell them to fack off, Joe!" said Strutter to the humongous six foot six black roadie.

Joe was like the fifth Cowboy, they split any money they got five ways. It wasn't the money Joe was really interested in though, he rarely paid for anything anyway, the opportunity to beat people into mush was the only reward he really required. Especially Germans. He loved beating Germans to within an inch of their Nazi lives. To Joe all war was going on everywhere - Vietnam, WW2 - all the time, now.

The drugs, psychedelics mainly, had scrambled him bigtime. Like a lot of roadies it was the large amounts of LSD and repeated viewings of Apocalypse Now that had done for him. It was an occupational hazard for crew. A lot of the lads lost it over that movie Das Boot - the German U-boat epic was dangerous film for the easily influenced footsoldiers of rock. That moody submarine flick did for whole swathes of road crews when it was first released on video. Repeat viewings, amphetamines and the rest, it's easy to imagine how those tour buses trundling along some deserted Scandinavian motorway at four in the morning could turn into a dank, fetid, stinking Nazi submarine trawling the depths of a hostile Atlantic. Das Bus fever it was called.

The poor bastard should have been in Broadmoor really. But regular doses of uncalled for gratuitous violence towards people he had never met before seemed to work like lithium for the gentle giant.

Joe yanked open the door and drew back his enormous fist. It was some butler type guy with a whole fucking trolley full of chicken, champagne, cold beers. bourbon, Polish vodka - all premium brands - caviar and all manner of deli-delectables.

"Courtesy of Mr Darklord, sirs" said Ballbag the butler.

"Nice one, Tramps!" shouted Strutter into the corridor, grabbing a hunk of chicken, eating the skin and throwing away the meat. Mince grabbed the rest of the chicken and stuffed his hand up the parson's nose, a big old shit-eating grin cracking his chops.

"Very nice one!" he grinned, pulling out fistfuls of plastic bags.

"Very fackin nice one! How's this for a cosmic turkey!"

he laughed, holding up a plethora of pharmaceutical goodies.

Dandelion Dandelion was touching up her pink lipstick in the ladies. She wanted to look her best, stand out from the rest of the rock chicks - which wouldn't be hard, most of them were old enough to be her mother.

She'd decided that tonight was going to be a very special night.

Tonight she was going backstage, she knew Mincey would know that she wasn't just another groupie road-hog. Tonight she was determined that glamorous troubadour, Mincey Harris was going to be hers. She just knew it.

Chapter Eight

The Gods Of Toxicity

To say that the Leather Cowboys were wasted does not even start to do justice to the royally fucked-up, pissed-up, coked-up, sideways cranked, pinned-down rolling mess of drugs and magic that shambled onto the small stage that night. The very fact that they could even see their instruments let alone play them can only be taken as definitive truth that the myths of the Gods Of Toxicity are true.

The Leather Cowboys played the gig of their lives.

Even the drum solo during 'Shitfaced' - a bone of contention between Robbie and the rest of the band for nearly 16 years - sounded godlike. Thor and his Valkyries danced on his skins, setting the place on fire with the groove-electric.

Amazing. What the fuck were they on that made them sound so...so cosmic? They'd dabbed, smoked, swallowed, snorted the whole fucking bag of goodies that Mincey had found up the chicken's arse but nothing they'd ever had before had made them play so fucking brilliantly. It was as if they were communicating telepathically, an 8 legged fucking groove machine. Strutter's solos took the top of your head clean off, leaving your scorched eyeballs spinning like planets in the gore. Gerry, the Mexican ex-wrestler bass player, had washed down his share of the chemicals with a whole bottle of silver tequila and, man, was that fatboy flying!

This was what rock'n'roll space age boogie was all about - what life was all about - thought Mincey as he saw Strutter puking up onto the audience. Mincey thanked the Gods Of Toxicity for keeping him on the rock'n'roll highway all these years, keeping his fire burning when it seemed the whole world was against them.

The band started jamming free style, a kaleidoscopic space metal boogie from the stars. Mincey was grooving cosmic, the words to songs he'd never even written pouring free-form stream of consciousness style from his mouth and they sounded both awesome and profound. They'd found the legendary cosmic groove and boy were they on it! The world was dayglo slowmo. Mincey smiled as he saw Joe wading into the audience, lashing out a la Sam Peckinpah, huge arcs of blood cascading across the monitors, wow.

The monstrous roadie was having the time of his slow motion life, smiling as he slammed around the audience, stoking mayhem.

That's when Mincey spotted the most beautiful girl he'd ever seen in his life, shining like an angel from heaven down there in the spew pit, untouchable and holy.

He recognized her from a lot of the other gigs they'd played but tonight, tonight she was beautiful. She smiled at Mincey as blood from one of the casualties of Joe's war splattered across her gorgeous face.

Mincey played the rest of the gig specifically for her, connecting in some far out cosmic way with the mystery girl, free associating these fantastic lyrics, gifts from the Gods of Toxicity.

Dandelion Dandelion felt it too.

"Tonight my love tonight, we two shall be one..."

The words came into her head from nowhere as she watched Mincey doing that sexy tongue flicking thing he always did. Her bumhole shivered in her knickers as she came like hydroelectricity.

Unless the whole audience were on whatever the Cowboys were on then they hadn't imagined it. They went back for three encores, finishing off with an extended cosmic version of 'Blow Job Queen'. Strutter seemed to levitate under the strobes and dry ice as he peeled off squealing hellfire and beautiful damnation from his flaming Gibson Explorer.

"Blowjob Queen, you know what I mean, she's outraaageous, yeah!!" bawled Strutter and Mincey into the same microphone.

The gutter twins.

Chapter Nine

Mott Slinging, Fanny Farting,
Spunk Burpers

Mincey was so high he was almost afraid he wasn't going to come down. His head felt like Hiroshima. He staggered backstage and out through the stage door. He wandered for what seemed hours but he knew from previous journeys in the 5th dimension that it was probably only minutes. He came to his senses for a second, wondering where the hell he was.

The silence of the dark Soho backstreet took a sinister twist, he could feel the underground train vibrating beneath the pavement, a nervous wave of panic gripped him as a rat skittered out from the rubbish at the back of The Rising Bunghole Sushi bar on Tottenham Court Road. The air smelled strange, like fried electricity. He reached in his back pockets for his works and shot up the last of his gear into his eye, the panic subsiding as the evil flowers worked their magic, flowing through his body like God's own medicine. That's when he saw the shadowy figure next to the bins. A faint blue nimbus surrounded the head of the black apparition.

"Please..." said the figure, stepping into the yellow pool of light, his face a mask of shadows. Mincey stepped back

"Please, Mr Harris, don't be afraid.."

Fear wasn't an emotion Mincey's medicine allowed but it was nonetheless there beneath the heroin detachment, a thin blue pulse like the onset of herpes.

"Yeah man, cool, what's up?" drawled Mincey - slow but not cool. The fear was there, just.

"I'm afraid you're in terrible danger ."

Mincey turned around to walk away. This cat was

deeply twisting his mellow.

He set off into the shadows but somehow the guy was still there in front of him.

"Listen, man!" said Mincey reckoning it was some queer out for a spam supper, "I'm pretty fucked up!"

He tried to pass the figure who was holding out a small white card.

"My number, for when you need it."
Not "if".
When...
Spooky!

Mince took the card just to get rid of him.

"Bill Drummond, Excromancer" read the card above a small ink drawing of what looked like a turd. Mincey looked at it and put it in his back pocket. The name sounded familiar but he couldn't place it. When he looked up the shadow had gone.

"Weird!" he muttered. Weird wasn't uncommon in Mincey's world. He shrugged and made his way back to the gig, forgetting the strange encounter almost immediately.

A flash of sheet lightning lit up the purple sky. Mincey didn't even notice.

The Leather Cowboys' front man walked back into the small cramped dressing room. The smoke from countless fags and heavily charged reefers cut visibility down to almost zero. The singer could hardly make out what all the grunting, undulating shapes in the toxic mire were up to.

"Shat the facking door man, I'm trying to get me facking marbles drained here!"

Mince recognised Strutter's deeply affected mockney accent. Strut was originally from a very respectable middle class background but amongst all the lies and self deluding mythopoeia they'd built around themselves, Strutter himself had even started believing he actually was an archetypal cockney guttersnipe, cor blimey, wotcher Guvnor.

'It's me, you kant!' said Mince "What the fack's going on? What's that facking smell! Jesus Christ, it's like a facking

Grimsby whorehouse!"

Mincey tripped over a seriously copulating Enchilada banging away on the floor - his fat, bean-farting Mexican arse pumping away grotesquely amongst the beer slop and fag ends.

Girlish giggles, farts and animalistic grunts echoed out of the smog, Mince felt an expert hand on his fly, fishing around in his leathers for his old man.

"Facking lapdancers, you kant!" shouted Strutter. "That facking Darklord geezer, he facking knows how to treat his support band!".

The smoke had cleared slightly and amongst the murk Mincey could make out the writhing forms of half a dozen silicon harlots fellating and taking it up the shitter, sliding around in baby oil and perversion all over the place.

Robbie the drummer had his face stuck to some blonde's arse, chewing away like an evil sucker-fish, mangling some poor lapdancers bumhole right through her rubber knickers.

Mince slapped the slut's hand away, his tackle wasn't in the healthiest state these days, he'd at least four STD's and a particularly grotesque fungaloid thing had taken root in his underpants. Even the blackhearted Mincey Harris couldn't bring himself to pass this particular strain of virulent bacteria on to anyone, not even this bunch of mott slinging, fannyfarting, spunk burpers.

Besides, his unusually accurate vibe antennae were still trembling around steadily escalating paranoid latitudes. This extra generosity of The Tramps only stoked his suspicions more. Mincey loaded a pint glass with a healthy cocktail of rum, bourbon, vodka and coke. The alcohol should take the edge off his trepidation he reasoned, wandering up to the side of the stage.

The Tramps of Dawn were just about to do their shit. The stage was pitch black, the winking LED's tantalising the expectant audience. An intro-tape kicked in, Mincey recognised the piece, it was 'Night On Bald Mountain' - the powerful

Rimski Korsakov piece celebrating the witches' Sabbat. It was effective, there's no doubting that, a genuine wave of uneasiness seemed to settle over the whole hall. The Tramps weren't holding back on the spectacle just because it was a small warm up gig. The macabre music started swelling to its ominous crescendo.

The bastards were using a different PA rig to what the Cowboys had been using. Mince smiled, realising that the noble Mr Darklord's hospitality knew its limit. In the time honoured tradition of support and main band sound levels, the Tramps were going to be at least three times louder than the support act.

A single spotlight picked out Darklord himself on the blacked out stage. He was a charismatic motherfucker, you couldn't take that away from him. His long, lank, raven coloured hair framed his white face. Coal black eyes, wild and untamed, laser-beamed into the audience. This was the it that Mincey had recognised in his fellow singer.

The eyes also were also possessed of that as well.

The thing Mincey knew he would never have.

Darklord's eyes possessed the terrifying spark of a zealot's mania.

Whatever dark world Peter Darklord conjured in the circumference of his charisma was more than real. It was black magic. His murderous gaze was possessed of the same burning demon manifest in the work of The Marquis de Sade. A cruelty borne out of terrible injustice and a rebellious spirit that craved far more than revenge.

Darklord's eyes were those of a man whose single desire was to be acknowledged an equal to God.

Where most men would conform to the dictates of an oppressor, Darklord's spirit would destroy the world before he would bend his knee to anything on Earth or in Heaven or Hell.

Darklord was possessed of a supernatural aristocracy as rare as it was awesome.

As beautiful as it was damned.

The man was the Devil himself.

Chapter Ten

Ten Inches of Biker Tube Steak

Dandelion Dandelion was shitting herself. She'd only ever seen pictures of the dark star, listened to the man's wild music. Being in the same room as him was fucking with her head bigtime. Her cunt was lubed up beyond anything she'd ever dreamed possible, the wet cooze pulsing in rivers down her young thighs. She wasn't the only one, the place stank of bitches in heat. The men in the audience were experiencing similar libidic insanities, sporadic coupling breaking out all over the place. Like animals.

A long sustained note from the lead guitar started undulating and taking on a sound she'd never heard before. It whooped and hollered, divebombing and screaming like a tortured baby.

Darklord started attacking his bank of synthesised mayhem, wrenching terrifying cacophonies from his overamplified short wave radios. It was the raw sound of a violent universe. Shattered galaxies and exploding supernovae. This wasn't just music, it was something else, a sound that connected to something primal in its listeners. Dandelion Dandelion had seen some wild audiences in her time, but nothing like this. This was more like mass hysteria, women tearing at their breasts and ripping out their hair in a black Dionysian frenzy. Men red in tooth and nail attacking each other like wild beasts. All the time the frenzied rhythms building and building, Darklord himself climbing his tower of synthesizers and radios, ripping out their wiry guts and attacking them with bloody fists.

Dandy could take no more, her head spinning like a whirlpool, hands grabbing her violently, ripping at her clothes, cocks coming at her from every angle, punching into every orifice. The pretty teenager passed out from lack of oxygen, choking on ten inches of biker tube steak, being buggered simultaneously by three security guards.

Mincey himself wasn't immune from the frenzied riot, he staggered backstage, his dick boning up like nothing he'd ever known in all his drug-addled years.

"Fack the fungus!" he muttered, falling dick-first into some hysterical lapdancer's face. It was as if he'd been plugged into some gut-grinding, sexually insane powerforce, hopping from choking mouths to bloody, torn arseholes and swollen cunts. The whole dressing room writhed and twisted like some horrific sexual inferno, pints of spunk and fanny batter splashing all over the walls, cunts and arseholes pulsating like in a horror movie. The screams and wailing way beyond anything orgasmic were shattering into primal regions of the soul long forgotten.

Chapter Eleven

Frankie Auschwitz

The after show party was held in The Himmler Hotel, a small, exclusive place tucked away in Mayfair. Mincey was against going to the party from the beginning.

The whole thing was getting weirder by the hour. The singer had tried to convince himself that the disturbing attack of priapic insanity during the Tramps' gig was a side effect of the mystery drug that Darklord had supplied them with amongst all the usual suspects.

The rest of the band had no such worries, they were quite happy to groove along on the atomic gonad rollercoaster. Buggering, fur sliding, wanking, being noshed, shooting out pint after pint of bollock snot in the back of the limo with the cockcrazed lapdancers. Mince pushed Strutter's arse out of his face angrily, the demon axe man was standing on the seats, slamming hard into a lapdancer's face, Mince noticed the needle hanging out of his arm.

"Facking speedball!" muttered the singer. Strutt usually only snorted the stuff. The degeneracy levels were creeping up on them. Mince cracked-up, the popping crystals turning into white smoke which he pulled deep into his lungs. His neurons started spinning as he slid up, up, up... into the gangsters' paradise, oh, yess, oh yessssss...

He could see the come down hanging around in the mists of euphoria over in the distance like a masturbating leper with a sack of bad news and a bag full of grind offal. Mince grabbed the needle from Strutter's arm and jabbed it into his eyeball before the leper could reach him.

The Leather Cowboys were vomited onto the pavement from the stretch, a gaggle of lapdancers with ripped clothes covered in sperm stains fell out after them, one poor girl hurled up her protein all down the back of Strutter's leathers.

"Strides baby, watch the strides!" said the touchy guitarist. He pushed her into the gutter where she continued hurling her spunky vomit and pubic hairballs.

The band were waved through the door of the Himmler Hotel by silverback gorillas in shades and dickybows. The lapdancers weren't. Which was cool with the Cowboys. They'd served their purpose and were promptly forgotten. Such is the lot of a slag.

"To abuse the holy power of the gash is a venal sin indeed." mused the Mincer as he noticed a couple of the lapdancers being taken into a side room, presumably to fellate their way into the exclusive bash.

"Sisters, when will you learn?" He shook his head and scoped the room, looking for dealers and young cunt. The heroin was charging him down, dissipating the paranoia, a couple more digs and a line of his Royal Highness and Mincey might even lighten up and enjoy himself. It was a long, long time since they'd experienced the kind of gratis Darklord was laying on for them. Mincey smiled, remembering the parties back in the Glam days, 1973 AD, when their star almost rose.

If it hadn't been for Gerry Enchilada, the Mexican macho nacho boy freaking out at some big record company party when he found out the little chicquita he'd been skeezing with all evening was packing a pound of sausalito and then tried to drown her in the toilet bowl.....Then again, how was the dumb beaner supposed to know that the little tranny arse bandit was the only son of Sparkling Anus Records MD Frankie Auschwitz. The record company bastards closed ranks after that.

And when the Cosmosodomistic Black Gas Corporation started muscling in on the whole industry, a lot of Mincey's peers hung up their bippety boppety hats and handed in their satin and tat. But not The Leather Cowboys, they were made of sterner, more erectile stuff.

They still believed in rock'n'roll.

The poor, deluded, glorious idiots...

Chapter Twelve

The King of Sodomism, Lord of all Perversions
under The Moon,
His Royal Felchness, High Fist Ubiquitous, Child Molester to
HRH The Queen,
the Fat Big Gareth

Dandelion Dandelion also loved rock'n'roll and, even though she was only sixteen, she was no groupie. She was in fact (was being the operative word) a virgin up until that moment of wild abandonment during The Tramps' earth shattering gig.

She'd enjoyed the intense orgiastic atmosphere, her throat was sore from the savage face-rape she'd enjoyed and her arse and cunt both felt as if they'd been ravaged by a troop of on- the-lam Broadmoor monkeys packing lawn mowers and fireworks.

Somehow, somehow it all felt right.

It was a manifestation, a rising. An ancient form of worship through blood letting and sacred jizz-snarfing, sacraments of a powerful Earth God.

It was, at least for Dandelion Dandelion, a pagan defloration.

Dandelion knew about the old Gods, her father's library was stacked with all manner of books detailing the beliefs, worship and customs of the decadent deitys of Ancient Greece and Rome. Many of the well-thumbed tomes in Latin and Greek, languages that her father had schooled her in for as long back as she could remember. As a child Dandelion had wiled away many long summer afternoons daydreaming of the lives of the fallible and often cruel and spiteful Gods of the Ancient world.

She believed that every aspect of the human psyche from the noblest forms of selflessness and generosity to the pettiest acts of spite and jealousy were to be found and understood in the myths focused around these deities. Like ancient soap operas. Their glories, failures, grand victories, and mad love affairs.

Somehow, she didn't know why but the idea of fallible divinity appealed to her.

It was Bacchus, that wild Roman God of booze and madness, that Peter Darklord and his music had somehow awoken. That dangerous wine drinker and fornicator, a lusty favourite of our sensual Mediterranean ancestors who liked nothing more than a fine, spunk-splattered, fanny-battered, shit-besmirched Bacchanalia.

That ultimate party-animal, Bacchus, along with his Greek predecessor Dionysus, had more or less claimed this rock'n'roll thing as their own. And who would, who could argue with that?

Dandelion was pleased that her maidenhead had been taken by a fellow reveller during the rising of the mad God and not by some fumbling boy with dirty nails and a knob the size of a field mouse.

In the afterglow of the airtight shafting Dandy felt changed, the gallons of jizz and foaming cooze that had spurted and pulsed throughout the Shit and Shovel had been her initiation into womanhood. Her confidence in her new found sexual maturity steeled her will. Tonight, Mincey Harris, she thought, you are mine!

She knew how to get into the exclusive debauch at the ultra-exclusive Himmler Hotel. Her mother used to tell her all about how you get to meet the big exciting rock stars.

Like an old pro, the confident teenager sucked off a couple of bow-tied gorillas and pulled off a roadie. The cloakroom boy who'd seen all of this pushed his luck and asked Dandy to fist him. Dandy obliged the cheeky little AC/DC horn smoker, but - when she was up to the elbow - she grabbed a slippery kidney and twisted hard. The diminutive chancer bastard screamed and fell to the ground, coughing bloody chunks all down his white shirt. Dandy smiled and wiped the shit off her arm onto the impudent punk's spiky hair.

Through a black velvet curtain embroidered with silver stars and dusted with purple glitter she stepped into the candlelit halls of rock'n'roll Babylon.

A great oyster of spunk splattered across her face.

High above the guest's heads, suspended in gold leather harnesses and swinging on silver trapezes, about thirty or forty dwarves were masturbating vigorously, throwing down their slimy jam like perverted seagulls. It seemed to be a game of some sort with people trying to catch the dwarves' emissions in their mouths. Dandy wiped the copious globs of deformo jizz from her black hair and scowled. She made her way through the crowded room of freeloaders pigging down on the caviar and champagne, snorting lines of cocaine from each others' naked breasts and straining bell enders.

One woman looked vaguely familiar. She was dressed in clothes reminiscent of the Pre-Raphaelites. Expensive hippy shit, layers of silks and beads, long corkscrew blonde hair drenched in dwarf jizz. She was bending over a table dreamily, her skirts pulled up around her waist as she pulled her arse cheeks apart while a seven foot tall black bloke wearing nothing but a gold turban blew cocaine up her arse with a rolled up fifty. The giant plugged her baggy sphinc with a couple of white doves to keep the drug firmly in place.

This was Dandy's first big rock party, of course she'd read about them but she'd never really believed the oft repeated tales of almost Roman depravity.

But here it was in all its intoxicated glory.

She recognised a lot of the people from pictures in magazines and newspapers. A sleazy looking guy that reminded her of a rat, not much taller than the sex dwarves and covered in exotic tattoos, was vomiting what seemed like twenty gallons of sperm all over a guy from another band whose name she couldn't remember. He was the singer in a poofy synth duo and was stuffing all kinds of exotic pets, pancake tortoises, gerbils, chinchillas and labrador puppies up his unsmiling friend's stretched jacksie.

Another creep from some American weirdy band, a tall guy dressed in a ridiculously large suit and Malcolm X glasses, tried to shit in her handbag, the cheeky, dirty bastard. He nearly managed it as well, nipping his stool off onto the floor and running into the crowd when confronted by an angry Dandy.

Of course no rock'n'roll debauch could ever be complete without the king of sodomism, the lord of all perversions under the moon, his royal felchness, the high fist ubiquitous, molester to HRH The Queen, Fat Big Gareth. There he was in the corpse blue flesh. Even Dandy knew the name of the king of buggery. Sat in a darkened alcove with his court of mincing fags, chicken hawks and their little chicks all buggering and fellating away in a tangled knot of anal confusion. The Fat Gareth thing allowed a small smile to flicker across his bloated features as an intravenous drip of hospital quality heroin and cocaine was stabbed up through the folds of his stomach into his jap's eye.

Dandelion was mesmerised by the sheer scale of perversity and buggerology sliding like madness all around her. She was unaware of course that the heady atmosphere was being helped along its grisly route by the amyl-nitrate fumes being pumped into the air from a petrol tanker parked around the back. The rushing sensations taking her up and down with the loud music were making her feel quite sick.

It was only when another load of dwarf sperm splattered all down the front of her tight white T-shirt, sparking her out of the druggy torpor, that she realised why she was there. Mincey Harris, her soul mate - it was written in the stars.

Another load of pearly spaz juice almost blinded her and she threw a beer bottle up at the repulsive three foot tall onanist, knocking him from his trapeze.

Chapter Thirteen

Scatalogical Cinderella

Mincey was high. The Leather Cowboy couldn't believe it.

It took prime quality speedballs to drag the jaded rocker from his usual gonnorheal pits of self-loathing and masturbatory despair. The only time Mincey ever felt alive these days was when he was rocking. Strutting the stage, banging his tambourine and shaking his grisly thing.

He'd almost forgotten what it was like. Mincey had been on a sustenance diet of his brown monkey drug for more years than he could remember. It took the edge off the sickness, stopped that metaphorical primate from chewing his guts up and turning him into a ball of nervous anxiety.

The singer had tried to quit dozens of times, but as soon as he got rid of one monkey a new one would take its place, and it was invariably that violent, incontinent, shit-black whiskey monkey, swearing all over the place and beating the living crap out of any woman stupid enough to be drinking with him.

At least his smack chimp didn't smash the house up and shit its pants.

Compared to the whiskey gorilla, his junkie monkey appeared almost benign. As long as it was fed that is. And even if it wasn't, the withdrawal symptoms from heroin had been greatly exaggerated. Heroin addiction, like alcoholism, was usually a symptom of some other problem. For junkies this was usually a lack of backbone and a tendency towards morbid self pity. The myth of cold turkey as metaphor for redemption was just another cockeyed invention of the literary softboys.

The cold turkey agonies these nances would have us believe they suffer are a total nonsense. Complete bollocks. The truth being that the withdrawal symptoms from heroin in most cases are no worse than a dose of pretty average flu.

Delirium Tremens, the alcoholic's ravaged turkey, however, is a whole different sack of pink elephant shit. Mincey remembers seeing one of his old roadies, Dogfart McBastard, jangling the dypso-jitterbug, shaking like a pneumatic road drill and jackknifing sideways into a grand mal, choking to death on his own tongue.

And Gorebladder, the chick drummer from the female metal band The Fuckpigs, drowning on her own blood. Fuck that shit!

Mince had decided that the demons determined to stop him from ever tidying up the chaos of his emotionally retarded life were a lot safer sedated with Paki brown than Tennants Super.

Mince had just hoovered up another half teaspoon of uncut Charlie and added to the raucous chorus of two hundred simultaneous monologues with a brilliant soliloquy of his own. Because of its purity, people were dropping like flies everywhere. These were dealt with swiftly by a couple of dwarves in cartoon doctors' outfits, mirror headbands, stethoscopes and jam-jar specs. The hallucinatory medics would drag the collapsed and bloody debauchees into another room so as not to bum out the rest of the high lifers. Peter Darklord was considerate like that.

Mincey was shouting at some chick who was shouting back at him when her nose exploded all down the front of her ridiculous cleavage, blood and pink jelly fucking everywhere. The dwarves had her out of there double-quick which was a bit of a pisser for the randiferous Mincer - the drug was working major bone size on the blood in Mincey's gristle hammer. Angry purple veins like knotted string were straining fit to burst on his quivering chopper. The Mince needed to unload his bollock-gravy big time. The evil snatch-salami thrashed around in his leathers like a great-white, hungry for cooze. Mincey felt his penis drawing him as if by magic towards the beautiful teenager stood perfectly still at the side of the room.

It was her. The girl from the gig.

The angel from the spew pit.

"My name's Dandelion Dandelion" she said, her earlier confidence waning by the second as she gazed into the Mincer's pinned bloodshot peepers. She bit her bottom lip and glanced nervously at her twisting hands, flickering her gaze this way and that, afraid to look the singer in the eye. Her teenage mott juiced up like a split fig, she could feel it running down the inside of her legs, her pubes as soggy as a rainy spaniel.

It was true love.

Mincey had her in the bogs in under a minute.

All the cubicles were empty so he did her in the urinal, the blocks of blue disinfectant caught up in her black hair looked like sapphires, the gutter of piss like a mountain stream. So lost in love were the frenzied couple that Dandy started coming as soon as her star-crossed hero slammed in the ham. The thought crossed Mincey's mind that the coke might render him unable to jizz, but so passionate was their wild rut that he spasmed almost immediately, great wads of jizzwater surging up the maddened girl, searching for the mysterious machinery of her sex.

"Oh Mincey!" she gasped covering his face with kisses, licking the piss off his face.

"Dandy!" he grunted, still thrusting gently, his dick still hard. He wiped the soggy cigarette butts from her tits and started chewing on her swollen nipples. Dandy couldn't seem to stop coming, wave after wave of wild sensations like dull electricity ebbing out from her cunt to every nerve-ending in her body, she felt like a giant orgasm falling through space. Her lover picked her up and threw her into a recently vacated cubicle, pushing her over the unflushed bog and jamming his super erotic piledriver up her teenage sphinc, ramming away like a frenzied mongrel, his long black hair whipping her on her back

"Oh yes Mincey! Yes! Yes!" she screamed. Driven to the

point of sexual insanity she grabbed the disintegrating furry-floater from the toilet bowl and started rubbing it in her hair and face. She was lost, lost in something animalistic, something animalistic and primal.

"Yes!" She screamed smearing her tits with the sloppy shite, sucking her fingers, licking it off, biting her knuckles.

"I LOVE YOU! I LOVE YOU! YOU FUCKING, FUCKING, FUCK PIG, BASTARD!"

Mincey carried on banging but the screaming was putting him off, he reached round and put his hand over her mouth, she started thrashing her head from side to side, banging her arse back onto his skinny thighs, making little yelping noises like a muffled puppy. Together, amongst the shite, used johnnies, fag ends and blue disinfectant, the star-crossed lovers melted into the universe as they both supernovaed into the ecstasy of a simultaneous orgasm, flickering silver lights, jump edit hyper-reality echoing white fire in their united souls.

"Facking 'ell!" breathed the Mincer, falling back against the door, leathers round his knees. "Facking 'ell" he breathed again, pulling out a broken Camel Light, sliding to the slopping floor and trying to find his mouth with trembling fingers.

"What a facking goer!" he managed to gasp between breaths. For Mincey that was the nearest he'd ever come to saying "I love you". Dandy snuggled up to her man, flicking the congealed faeces and soggy bog roll from her hair as if they were daisies. They burst into intimate giggles when they heard some party animal unloading a collosal, farting, splashing dump in the next door khazi.

As their heartbeats slowed down to a less fevered pace, that fat rat, grim reality started poking around the corners of their dream.

Turds, piss, johnnies, fags.
Poor Dandy, she fled in terror.
A scatalogical Cinderella.
Leaving behind her a shit stained tampon instead of a

glass slipper.

Mincey, who wasn't totally unused to this kind of stuff looked confused.

The singer searched high and low for the magical girl, but she'd vanished.

Like a fart.

The saddened Mincey, lovingly fingered the soiled jamrag in his leather pants pocket.

"Dandy!" he mouthed silently, a hole inside him starting to ache.

The beautiful girl had stolen his heart.

Chapter Fourteen

Dwarf Sperm

"Mr Darklord will see you now, sir," said the immaculate flunky.

Mincey didn't hear him, an unfamiliar emotion was tearing at his insides.

Twenty years of hard rocking had numbed the singer's finer sensibilities. The lovestruck dope was confused, his emotional landscape was so ravaged by hard drugs and appalling debauchery he couldn't understand what had happened to him. For Mincey, all sensation was wrapped up in a vocabulary that described all feelings in terms of its nearest narcotic equivalent.

Never having previously experienced love he couldn't figure out what it was that he was jonesing for.

"Sir," repeated the flunky. "Mr Darklord is waiting for you. Are you feeling unwell, sir?"

Mincey saw the staid butler for the first time

"Some heroin, perhaps? Mr Darklord has some excellent China White, a vintage stock I believe."

The mention of the excellent synthetic heroin grabbed the singer's attention.

"Yeah, yeah..." said the Mincer, miles away.

"And crack, yeah some crack, straighten me out.."

"I believe Mr Darklord has some first rate freebasing facilities, sir..." said the flunky, stewarding Mincey through the apocalyptic debauchery sliding all around them.

"A first rate performance by the way, sir, 'Blow Job Queen', most rocking."

Most rocking? Who the fuck was this cat? This shit's

getting very LSD, thought the Mincer. What's happening? His paranoia wobbling - the China White would sort him out. The lure of serious mellow focused the confused degenerate. His lover's balls forgotten for a second, Mincey's main-monkey had woken up and it needed feeding. A glob of dwarf sperm landed on his sleeve, he wiped it off absent mindedly.

"Wanking dwarves," he smiled, "haven't seen that since the '70s..."

The baroque Peter Darklord was sat on a modest throne at the end of a shadowy antechamber. He was theatrically pulling on a large ornate silver hookah, the blue smoke swirling dramatically around his sharp aristocratic features. Mincey suppressed a bemused smile, trying to curl his lips.

What an arsehole! he thought. But Mincey couldn't deny that the black robed figure cut an extremely elegant shade of decadent twat.

Darklord passed the pipe to an unsmiling child dressed only in precious stones. There was no denying that the mysterious Mr Darklord was possessed of a beautifully realised Baudelairean aesthetic. The elegant dandy rose to his feet and seemed to glide towards him holding out a long bejeweled hand. Mincey unexpectedly found himself charmed by the warmth of his host's smile.

"Mr Harris," said the smiling aesthete, "or may I call you Mincey?"

The Mincer couldn't help liking the guy, he was just one of those blokes that you took to instantly, his honesty and openness winning you over despite his ludicrous affectations. Besides, thought The Mincer, who am I to talk about fucking affectations!?

Mincey instinctively understood that Peter liked dressing up and make believe as much as he did himself.

"Listen, Pete, man," said Mince, "all that shit I said in Metal Bumhole, whatever the fuck it's called, you know, man, just a fackin' laugh, I didn't mean it or nothing."

Mincey assumed that Darklord perused every scrap of information written or said about him in the music press.

In this respect Darklord was genuinely aristocratic in his manner, never reading anything written about himself but occasionally asking a flunky who was employed solely to read the scribbled nonsense churned out by the subnormal gentlemen of the musical press to summarise the general flavour of this nonsense.

"Mincey, dear boy, I rarely read anything written about myself. I'm surely not going to read anything about, if you forgive me, your dear self. I'm sure you're the same. Anyway, we're not here to talk shop, please, forgive me, it is heroin isn't it? I have some excellent China White? Or perhaps a little brown? I have a man in Karachi..."

Peter's Chinese manservant entered silently. The small Chinaman - dressed in traditional silken robes, complete with pigtail and wispy beard - placed a tray containing two bowls of prepared heroin. A small, solid silver hypodermic lay in a lacquered box lined with velvet. Mincey had copped a few degenerate aristo's works before, shared them before all this AIDS shit, but he'd never clapped eyes on a set of works this fine. The silver was inscribed with all manner of intricate occult designs. He plunged up the juice. It was 100% - that was evident by the faint blue gleam that only pure China White gave off. Mincey pardoned himself and banged himself up in his left eyeball.

The shit even gave him a vague rush. He couldn't remember the last time that had happened. The rocker almost felt good. The Chinaman returned with a small silver tray laden with a generous supply of crack cocaine. The Mince piped up. The shit was fucking good, up, up, up, oh yessss, gangster's paradise, baby ...oh fuckfuckfuckfuuuuccckkkk....

"Bollinger I think, or Kristal, possibly with crack, Mincey?" said the perfect host.

"Have you any beer?"

"Certainly, Wang Chung, an ice cold Tennents Super

for Mr Harris, if you please."

"And 80 Camel Lights, mate, if you don't mind, that is..." added the Mincer, his nicotine addiction sent flaming by the crack.

Peter watched the Leather Cowboy sate all four addictions simultaneously with a polite detachment. He gave a courteous smile and nod when Mincey tried to focus on his host's face within the brief but delicious delirium of the fucked up gangster's paradise.

Chapter Fifteen

The Sodomy of Christ

Dandelion Dandelion had been in the shower for nearly an hour. The water had started to run cold but the distraught girl hadn't noticed. All she could smell was shit. She couldn't get rid of the stench. What had happened back there at the Himmler Hotel?

Her emotions were spiralling out of control, a deep and destructive love had been seeded in her soul. A love that no matter how dreadful and disturbing rejected all attempts to jettison the black flower. Her teenage cunt throbbed and dribbled at the memory of Mincey battering away behind her, a stranger's kak smeared all over her face.

God, what was wrong with her. Am I a pervert? she wondered.

Dandelion finally stepped out of the shower and decided to become a nun.

The Poor Sisters of Infinite Suffering welcomed Dandelion Dandelion to the cloistered fold.

The first few months passed quickly, Dandy worked and prayed hard, studying the Catechism. Dandelion's faith however was not as stable as she would have liked. Her father's gods were still there, waiting for her when she fell asleep. The whole salacious pantheon of goat legged priapic masturbators and flying winged peni fucking her in her dreams.

In a confused attempt to rid herself of all the filth locked up inside her unconscious mind Dandy threw herself ever deeper into the Catholic faith, the poor girl was quite unaware of the dark sexuality and lascivious sensuality that lurked deep at the Roman core of the Catholic church.

When the Mother Superior was confident that Dandy was both religiously competent and strong in faith she led the purified teenager into the Santa Sanctorum of the order of the Poor Sisters of Infinite Suffering - a locked and secret altar beneath the southern walls of the nunnery.

"In here, Sister Dandy, you will find the inspiration for our order of Infinite Suffering," whispered the Mother Superior.

"As you have learned over these seven months of prayer and contemplation, we are an elect order and, after you have gazed upon the holiest of our relics, we will expect a vow of eternal silence."

Dandy didn't know quite why but a sick dread descended upon her - a cloying sensation she could feel upon her skin like a film of cheap cooking oil.

This was the first she had heard of any vow of silence.

"The Forever Silence," said the Mother Superior. "The reason for this extreme act of submission towards our redeemer shall become apparent after you have seen our Chamber of Holy Relics And Icons".

Dandelions sphinc shivered. This was getting spooky.

She stepped into the dark chamber. There was a familiar smell.

Lubed cunt.

Dandelion was confused.

It wasn't her.

The Mother Superior was lighting the fat tallow candles which threw dancing shadows across the limewood effigies hung upon the walls and lurking in every corner. It was the usual collection of martyred saints - bleeding sores, gouged out eyes and shattered limbs all proclaiming the strength and unshakeability of their faith.

St Catherine broken on the wheel, Ignatius burnt alive, Sebastian the bumboy kebab - the walls were dripping with crude depictions of the saints and martyrs. All of them seemingly trying to outdo the Nazarene's agonizing end.

Dandelion detected a sickening sensuality in the suffering of certain saints, the fey Sebastian in particular, was that an erection behind his muslin jocker?

And the martyred nuns, was that agony or ecstasy upon their faces as the flames licked around their thighs?

Stripped sisters being whipped upon their full breasts till the blood dripped down and soddened the black hair between their virgin legs...

"You have progressed well, Sister Dandelion," said the Mother Superior, leading her young charge into the sinister shadows at the end of the room. Dandelion's nostrils twitched, the smell of suppurating fanny seemed to be getting stronger. She thought she could detect movement in the shadows

"Very well indeed..." the boss nun whispered in her ear as her hands started to remove Dandelion's robes. Dandy sighed as the old woman started to fondle her breasts. The shadows approached, about six or seven of them, one fell between young Dandy's legs and started chowing down on her sanctified clam. She surrendered and started popping off her multiples, coming like a machine gun, moaning like an American. One of the nuns pushed her across the altar and started buggering her. It took Dandy a few moments to realise what was happening, she pushed herself backwards

"Stop, stop! In the name of Christ stop!"

It was too late. Even Jesus couldn't save her. She had to face facts, she was a dirty cunt and she loved it. Aroused to gash-flooding hysteria she turned around and grabbed her sodomist's strap-on, fastening it to herself in a frenzy. Dandy started ripping off her fellow nun's habits and buggering the beatified bitches as they'd never been buggered before, spurting great gloops of St Peter's snake oil into her sisters' sanctified bungholes and then reaming them straight to pervoid heaven.

"Oh yes! Sister Dandelion! Its true! I knew you were the one! Our prophet and leader!" shouted the Mother Superior ecstatically

"What the fuck are you talking about, Batman?" Dandy

returned, banging hard on Sister Caroline's saintly shitter.

"The prophesy! Our Lord, the Thirteenth Station Of The Cross!"

The shattered but utterly sexually satiatied Mother Superior unplugged herself and, staggering like a lottery-winning alkie dosser after his 199th can of Tennants Super, started lighting the giant candles around the altar, revealing a terrible painting twenty feet tall and twice as wide. The grim and blasphemous rumour mentioned in the lost Apocrhypha, the book of Enoch from The Bible - it was true.

There in the sickly candlelight, the terrible painting by Goya of The Sodomy Of Christ.

Longinus, the Roman spearboy banging away on the holy hippy's sacred ringpiece like there was no tomorrow. In the background, hanging by his neck, the traitor Judas swinging in the breeze. Mary Magdalene snarfing deep on his dead boner while the Virgin herself, wearing a monster strap on, buggers the saintly prozzie's savagely stretched sphinc.

Chapter Sixteen

The Tijuanna Arse Cannon

The British leg of the Tramps' world tour turned out to be the last for Mincey and the boys. Disaster struck.

To say that Mincey took it badly would be the understatement of the century.

Strutter Sandanista had quit The Leather Cowboys and joined The Tramps Of Dawn.

After 20 years of hard rocking with Mincey, Gerry Enchilada and Robbie, the lousy, mercenary cocksucking bitch had quit The Cowboys and taken up with that creepy goth bastard Peter fucking Darklord and his shit eating, cocksucking Tramp motherfuckers.

No wonder the bastard Darklord had been so generous! The skink eyed fucker! He'd had it planned from the beginning!

Mincey's paranoid-antennae had been right all along.

The night Strutter unpacked the bombshell it was as if he'd never known them.

The drugs from the end of tour party hadn't even worn off when the treacherous Strutt walked into The Broken Arms pub on Kilburn high road and told them he was quitting the band and joining those faggots, The Tramps Of Dawn. A bolt of thick, blue electricity thumped Mincey hard in his solar plexus. He thought he was dreaming. No matter what had happened in Mincey's catastrophic, sexually-transmitted disease of a life, the band had been the one constant. The only thing he trusted and had any faith in. Women were treacherous and despicable creatures, not all of them of course, but the fickle fish that swam in the miasmic cesspools of rock certainly were.

Mincey felt hot tears sting his cheek. Strutter had been like a brother, like a wife, a noble friend and trusted companion during these past twenty years of desperate privations and bad rocking.

Gerry Enchilada's reaction was less sentimental. He pushed his all-day breakfast off the table, sending beans and sausages flying all over the place, and punched Strutter full in the face, knocking him flat on his arse into the vomit and fag ends. Hitching his tight bootcut jeans up over his builder's arsecrack the Mexican fatboy strolled around the table, belched loudly, bent at the knee slightly, cracked out a razzler and started giving Strutt the cowboy boots. Gerry had been drunk for 20 years or so, so his kicks didn't deliver much damage.

Robbie, as confused and hurt as the rest of them, helped Strutter back to his feet and wiped the blood from the guitarist's face. Gerry carried on attacking some other poor fucker stood innocently at the bar, thinking he was still laying into the treacherous guitarist. Twenty years of cheap tequila had finally got to his eyes, the fact that the Tijuana arse cannon never removed his skinny shades, day or night may have also contributed to this mistaken identity stomping.

"Why, man?" choked the Mincer, unable to control his emotions. "The Cowboys? Doesn't that mean anything to you?".

The Mincer knocked back his rum and coke and ordered a bottle of Captain Morgan. Fuck it. This situation was going to require some serious drinking, He ordered two bottles.

"I don't know, man," said Strutter, "maybe I don't believe in us anymore, maybe the Indians have finally beaten me. It's like, how many arrows can a man's heart take?".

Strutter's eyes were damp. This wasn't easy for him either.

"Don't believe in The Cowboys....!?" gasped the Mincer, incredulous, the lump in his throat almost choking him.

"Mincey, we've been rocking for 20 facking years, man, and through all that time I ain't never had enough money to pay my phone bill without it getting cut off. Living in facking squats and on people's floors, I've been signing-on for 20 years, Mincey! I can't take it no more!"

"So that's it, is it, Judas? You sell out your facking buddies for 40 pieces of facking silver! Facking money! Strutter? Strutter Sandinista?! A facking breadhead! I've facking heard everything now!" shouted the Mince, almost hysterical, choking back a ridiculously generous shot of rum.

"It's my lady, man, Guinnivere, she's up the duff, we're gonna have a kid, man. A little facking Strutter, he can't live off facking rider food like we do, can he? I can't put bags of crisps and M&Ms, and facking JackfackingDaniels in the facking blender can I?" argued Strutter desperately.

"We could get baby food on the rider man, no problem!" answered Mincey, clutching at straws, realising it and hanging his head, shock and rum connecting and stupefying him.

"So go on, how much have you sold us out for?" sulked the singer, his hands shaking as he lit his Camel Light.

"Forty grand a week," mumbled Strutter, ashamed. "But it's not just the money, Mince, look at the state of us, man, you're nearly 50, I'm 42 next week, Mince, I know you can't admit it, man, but we missed the boat, man, missed the facking space ship, whatever, I'm sorry man. I had to think about the baby...."

Strutt wiped a tear away from his eye.

"We're gonna name it after you if it means anything, Minceena if it's a girl, shit, man I'm so sorry, I'm gonna miss you Mince, miss all of you, even that fat Mexican arsehole over there'" he said, nodding in the direction of the drunken Mexican booting all hell out of a total stranger. Strutter held out his fist timidly.

"Get the fack out of here, man!" said Mincey, punching Strutter's fist gently, wiping a tear on the heel of his other hand. The baby's name was a nice touch.

"Don't be a stranger, man, now you're a big rock star.." Mincey laughed as Strutter turned to walk away.

"Oh yeah..." he called after Strutter, "and tell that Darklord cunt that I meant every word I said in Metal Bumhole. The guy's a tosser! Now go on fack off before I turn fatboy over there loose on you....".

Mincey laughed through his tears. Hate was not an emotion he had time for. It burns up the person doing the hating far more than the person being hated, that was a fact.

"What's he facking doing?" laughed Mincey, pointing at the perma-blasted, short sighted Mexican kicking the shit out of some poor guy over by the jukebox.

"That cat's got to go to the opticians man. Fack me!" said the Mince knocking back a fat rum.

Chapter Seventeen

Bumhole Through The Knickers

As if it wasn't bad enough with Strutter quitting the band, Mincey had been unable to stop thinking about the incident in the khazi with the Dandelion Dandelion chick. He couldn't seem to take his mind off the angelic teenager. Sure it had been a bit gruesome with the floater and all that. But everyone knows that passion, stoked correctly, can whip anything up into an erotic, spermo cyclone, even a floater. Well that's what it said in the skid magazines he had under his mattress anyway.

Mincey stuffed the tampon Dandelion had left behind her up his left nostril and started banging the crap out of his vinegar stick, spazzing into jizz mode and spunking all over the wall and filling his bellybutton.

Maybe Strutter was right? Maybe it was time for them all to quit the rock? Mincey could entertain the thought but he knew it would be impossible, it was ingrained too deeply into his soul. His blood was pumped by a heart that had a rock'n'roll beat.

Besides what else was he going to do? What else could he do?

Mincey decided that although he was never going to be able to hang up his leather strides maybe the time was right for a little break from the rock.

He desperately wanted to find Dandelion, the girl had touched a part of him that usually only the most transcendental incidents of rockness had ever touched.

A relative innocent in the minefield that is love, Mincey

would find her, of that he was sure.

He spent a week or so searching around all the salubrious rock joints in Soho - The Intrepid Rat, The Shit and Shovel, Bogwankers, The Rip Off And Buggery Club in Wardour street, Anal Confusion, The Sub and Mong, The Masturbating Teenager - but he wasn't having any luck at all.

Since he'd started his creepy love affair with the needle over 18 years ago, Mincey had more or less given up any serious dalliance with the fairer sex. There'd been the odd blowjob or group fisting sessions with the more persistent roadhogs but that was all.

But somehow the khazi incident had woken things in the Mincer that he'd long forgotten. Mincey had almost given up, he'd been trawling the pukey clubs and bars of the rock demi monde for over a month without any luck. It was as if she'd never existed. Fingering the gruesome jamrag in his leathers' back pocket, Mincey finished his pint of truly dreadful English lager and headed out into the loveless Soho night. He bought a doner kebab on his short walk to his grim flat. His heroin habit seemed to be slowing down, the kebab was the second thing he'd eaten that day. This love shit was messing around with his nervous system in ways that he'd never suspected.

The lightbulb in his bathroom was long gone so the 45 year old rocker was sat in the darkness ridding himself of a remarkably full load when the idea came to him. Of course, why hadn't he thought of it before!?

Dandelion Dandelion hadn't missed a gig in over five years. Whenever the Cowboys played, Dandy was there. Even when she was revising for her GCSE's the beautiful teenager managed to make the gig, writhing in the spew pit, lost in her own world, dreaming of the Mincer sucking on her bumhole through the knickers.

The Cowboys would rock again!

Love would be Mincey's.

Yeah.

Chapter Eighteen

Dribbling Perversion

Dandelion Dandelion was finished with The Poor Sisters of Infinite Suffering.

The whole idea of becoming a nun was to help her forget the grotesque floater incident in the mens toilets at the Shit and Shovel. But these nuns? Dandelion was having her doubts. No matter how passionate and full of secret sensuality the Bible was, all this strap-on lesbian buggery and clamdiving, surely this wasn't what the Nazarene intended up there on that Hill? But the painting and the hidden Apocrypha the Mother Superior had shown her whilst trying to fist her lungs out? What did it all mean? Dandelion was confused. Yes she was flattered by the order's declaration that she was the new Messiah and, compared with the wild scenes of sexual insanity that spermed all over her father's Pagan pantheon, this buggery business was almost cute in comparison.

Dandelion thought that the sisters' interpretations of the gospels were no wilder than many of the other demented, heretic offshoots of the church. All manner of sexweirdness had sprang from the holy bellend up there on his cross at Golgotha. The established church's interpretations were but one pearl of the sacred and holy cocksnot.

But if Dandy had wanted dribbling perversion and sore shitlockers, the Gods of Greece and Rome provided more than enough of that - incest, bestiality, Mother and Fatherfucking, donkeyshagging, cannibalism - you fucking name it.

But more than anything else she couldn't stop thinking of Mincey and the wild bone she had ridden in his arms.

"Oh Mincey!" she whispered to herself, giving her teenage clit a sly nudge. "Even Jesus himself couldn't steal my love from you."

She would leave that night, straight after the 7 o'clock prayer and buggery session.

There were worse things in the world than coprophilia.

Even though she couldn't think of any at the moment.

Chapter Nineteen

Teenage Junkie Bone Rider

The auditions for Strutter's replacement weren't going well. Rock's walking wounded stumbled drugily into Fat Arsed Frank's Kings Cross rehearsal studios. All of them reeked of alcohol and desperation. There was no doubt about it, rock'n'roll was a cruel mistress. Once that bitch had bitten you there was no escape. How many dreamers had sacrificed their lives on that sparkling altar of electric dreams? In they filed, clutching their battered guitars, plugging in and wangbarring their way through their fatfingered repertoire. The poor fuckers, most of them couldn't even get jobs as mini cab drivers let alone a gig with the Cowboys, their nerves were so shot by the road, cheap drugs and truly appalling sex. These desperados would have had difficulty even knowing which side of their instrument to play, never mind rocking out to the levels of blitzed insanity the Cowboys demanded.

Mincey and the boys' spirits were swilling desperately low when in he sauntered. He couldn't have been more than sixteen years old. Bitch mistress Rock had bitten him but unlike his older amigos she hadn't drained him. He plugged in his Les Paul deluxe sunburst finish and raised the Devil. The kid was a fucking genius. He knew all the Cowboys' songs; 'Cocksucker Strut', 'Buggering The Devil', 'Blow Job Queen', Boning In The Wreckage, 'Wanking in Japan', 'Arsebandit Apocalypse', 'Get Your Cock Out' - the kid peeled into all of them, keeping to Strutter's basic riffs but adding some devastating white-hot fretwork of his own.

Gerry, Robbie and Mincey looked at each other, smiling. 'What's your name kid?" asked Mincey, offering the youngster a can of Tennants Super.

"Sonny, sir.," said the young axeraper, pulling the top off the purple tin.

"Sonny Darklord."

The silence in the room was disturbed only by the electric hum from the kid's Marshall stack, it twisted gently around the bad smell of the funky rehearsal room. A full minute passed before anyone dared disturb the sacred buzz.

"Sonny Darklord?" said Mincey.

"That's right, sir. I think you know my dad, Peter Darklord..."

Gerry dropped his can of Tennants Super, unhooked his bass and took a clumsy swing at the fresh faced teenager, missed by a yard and fell flat on his beaner arse.

"I know you must think me auditioning for you is a bit weird but, believe me, there is no love lost between me and my old man," stuttered the son of Darklord nervously.

The Mexican stumbled to his feet, swearing and farting loudly. The burrito in his back pocket had splattered all over his arse. It looked like he'd shat himself.

"So what's the deal?" said Mincey, intrigued.

"I hate him, sir" said the handsome blonde teenager, flicking his long fringe from his eyes. "He's a fraud and a buggerist."

The kid gave a manly pull on the treacly 9% tramp water. "And I thought there was a nice twist, Strutter taking up with my old man, me joining his favourite band..."

He hit the can hard again, there was obviously nothing wrong with the kid's liver .

"Hang on a minute, his favourite band, us? The Cowboys?" said the Mince, cracking open his fifth can of derelict's ruin that morning.

"Yeah, he'd never tell you though. How do you think I can play all of Strutter's guitar parts note perfect, it's all the old cunt ever listens to. I've been listening to the Cowboys' music ever since I can remember." Sonny slashed off a spectacular guitar lick, his fingers blurring into the instrument's beautiful ebony neck..

Mincey's paranoid antennae weren't twitching. The kid seemed to be telling the truth.

"What's the beef with the old man" He said, offering him another can of bum puke

"Oh just the usual tabloid depravity stuff, my old man, he's so concerned about the Zeitgeist, he's terrified of losing touch with the real world, he has to go along with every quirk and bubble that surfaces from fashion's sleazy cess pool. He gets it wrong all the time though, that's why when I was seven the fucking idiot started using my arse like a dartboard, bumming me stupid every fucking night. He'd been reading all that paedophile stuff in the Sun and thought he was missing out on something, fucking bastard. He'll go fucking nuts if he finds out I've joined The Leather Cowboys."

Mincey laughed.

"Sonny Darklord, welcome to the strange world of The Leather Cowboys. Do you do heroin?"

He threw a fatherly arm around the handsome lads slim shoulders.

"Yeah man I've been on the needle since I was ten years old, it stopped my arse hurting," replied Sonny, pulling up his sleeve to show his bruises. "Oh and by the way," he continued, pushing his floppy blonde fringe from his eyes, "there's something else I think you should know."

The fey lad hesitated slightly.

"I'm a bummer, does it matter? I mean The Cowboys are quite a macho outfit so does my penchant for hornsmoking and being slammed up the dirtbox bother you at all? It's dad's fault, all that child abuse shit, it made me grow up weird".

Sonny cracked another Tennants Super.

"Don't be stupid kid," said Mince reassuringly. "The Cowboys are a lot of things but we aren't homophobic - in fact your bone riding skills might come in handy on long drunken tours, eh Gerry?"

The greasy, unshaven Mexican smiled, revealing his gold teeth. Gerry Enchilada would fuck anything with a heartbeat. He rubbed his thick black stubble and appraised the slim young man lecherously.

"Oh Si Senor, focking Si focking Senor!". The greasy pervert laughed, grabbing his crotch and making horrible buggery movements from his filthy armchair.

All four Cowboys cracked open the Tennants Super and made a frothing toast to themselves before careering into a searing rendition of 'Arsebandit Apocalypse', from their classic 70's album 'Eat My Shit', Sonny joining in on the chorus vocals just like Strutter used to.

"Arse bandit Apocalypse, yeah, yeah, yeah, alright"

Chapter Twenty

Turd Sex

Dandelion Dandelion felt a wave of relief wash over her as she stepped from the front door of the weirdo buggery convent. She had over-reacted ridiculously about Mincey and the floater incident, that was plain to her now. Six long months she'd wasted amongst the dildos and crucifi - the sperm of Christ indeed! The incredible energy and intricacy some perverts extend to realise their fetishtic abnormalities almost defied belief.

Sitting on the top of the number 19 bus to her mother's Clerkenwell flat, Dandy couldn't help thinking about Mincey. His long hair lashing across her back as he banged away like a madman riding a wild horse. The wet electric orgasm as if they were falling through the universe. She tried to forget about the floater.

As she stepped off the bus at Theobalds Road a small flyer pasted over all the other crappy flapping scraps of paper caught her eye. It was for The Cowboys, they were playing that night at The Fart and Chicken in Camden. She glanced at her watch, in just over two hours.

Dandy raced through the Bourne estate, if she hurried she could just about make it. Her heart was pounding like a gay disco.

She threw on her rock chick gear; black mini skirt, black stilleto heels and a tight white T shirt with a picture of the cover of the 1979 Cowboys album 'Slut'. Dandy loved the picture of Mincey and the boys in prostitute drag. If you looked real close you could see Mincey's penis, obviously erect, beneath the rubber skirt. The band were all quite young then, Mincey had a real androgynous look about him - the same look that'd been turning Dandy to water ever since her first period. She'd been rubbing her cunt dry for over five years fantasising about the man and the first time her dreams were turned into reality she'd joined a fucking nunnery! If Mincey was into turd sex then she'd have to get used to it. Dandy applied a pink slash of lipstick to her lips trying to make her mouth look as much like her cunt as possible. She'd read in Just Pubescent, the popular girls magazine, that that's what most boys dug about a chick. She'd been practising her blowjob technique for three years on cucumbers, bananas, lollypops. If that's what it took to get her man she was determined to suck Mincey's very soul out through his bell-end.

Her dad had been great about her sex education, he was really helpful, letting her suck on his real knob, to perfect her technique. He was real considerate as well, not spunking in her mouth or anything. Not many girls had such cool dads, she was lucky that way.

Dandy jumped on the tube at Kings Cross. On the short journey to Camden two business men flashed at her, she must be looking hot. Usually it was only one or two a week. Dandelion was always flattered by these mashing displays, taking it as a compliment, sort of like a wolf whistle, only one louder. She couldn't understand why other girls her age were so freaked out by these underground turkey spankers. They were quite sweet really, stood there crosseyed, tongues lolling out of their contorted faces, battering all mighty hell out of their monkey spanners in appreciation of a lady's charms and squirting their watery spud juice all down their crusty pants.

Dandelion found it funny when she tried talking to them, especially when a look of absolute terror crossed their twitching faces as they scuttled off the train at the very next stop.

Her heart was beating madly as she rushed up the broken escalator. She recognised a few diehard Cowboys fans obviously making their way to the gig past the ragged slaves of the purple tin. Every time Dandy visited Camden - London's answer to Amsterdam - the ranks of the derelict seemed to have swollen. There were about 40 of them this time, all sucking hard on that dreadful purple tin like babies on the tit. Wild white hair blown into mad shapes by the foetid breath of their own personal hells. Gesticulating grandly like little emporers of the gutter. Rolling around in spastic slow-motion drunken brawls, egged on by their brain-damaged fellow revellers.

It was the women Dandy felt sorry for, there was nothing worse than the stench of a derelict woman - unwashed gash clogged up with all manner of wild yeast infections and sanitary insanity. Crud stained knickers stiff with irregular menstruation and diarrhoea.

Dandy's mother used to do voluntary work, helping the homeless, that's how she met her dad. One of the bums had tried to rape her. Her dad, who was going through a bad patch and was also a street drinker, had pulled the rapist off her mother. The two became lovers shortly after. Dad got himself together and soon after little Dandy was born. Dandy handed one of the quieter casualties a pound coin and hurried up Parkway to The Fart and Chicken, her cunt was lubing up already and she hadn't even set eyes on her dreamboat yet.

Dandelion was in luck, the support band - a bunch of demented Finnish punk rockers called The Fuckers - hadn't even finished yet. They were energetic to say the least, chugging greedily on huge bottles of White Star cider in between songs with titles like 'Sexy Roy Orbison' and 'Burn Helsinki Burn'. Of course, being punk rockers the whole thing ended in a chaotic and violent fight with the audience. Being Finnish they hadn't realised that gobbing on your audience wasn't even considered cool when Captain Sensible used to do it over 20 years ago. Fortunately the Cowboys' massive roadie waded in to sort it all out, that mad grin hanging on his face as he pummelled the tiny little Finnish punks into reindeer meat. He picked all four of them up, one in each massive fist and the other two kicking and screaming under his muscley arm. The black behemoth took them backstage, a few minutes later the unmistakable sounds of sodomy torture could be heard out at the front of house.

Dandy put some more pink cunt lipstick on and moved through the small crowd at the front of the stage, she was wearing a wonderbra that pushed her tits up beneath her chin. Her cunt was in a real lather, nipples erect beyond belief, if they stiffied up anymore they were going to rip through her T shirt.

The lights went down quickly and then, in a blast of white light and a burst of smoke, there they were.

Dandelion came in her knickers, pissing herself for good measure.

Mincey looked fantastic, he did his rooster strut to the front of the stage, hands on his hips, head going back and forward like the cockiest cock on the block. Cock rock she thought spasming into another pant wetting orgasm. The singer saw her and immediately started doing his tongue thing, flicking it in and out as if he were licking her bumhole through her knickers. Another orgasm juddered through her. Dandelion didn't even notice the new guitar player until he joined Mincey on the mike for the chorus of 'Arse Sniffer'. He was extremely handsome and very young. And somehow his guitar playing sounded louder than Strutter's, if that was possible.

Dandy was in heaven. After the show, Mincey Harris - she thought - you're mine, turd sex or not.

She came again.

Chapter Twenty One

Rock'n'roll Fatwa

Mincey grabbed the mike.

"This next one's a new one, we wrote it last night, it's about that facking, baggy eyed cant, Salmon Pastie, whatever the fack he's called! How can that facking nonce write a facking book about rock'n'roll when he's never rocked in his facking life?!"

The crowd cheered, despite the fact that most of them hadn't a clue who Salman Rushdie was.

"Just because he's hung out with those facking Irish facking bogwogs, Bonio and his garden facking hedge, whatever fack they're called as well...".

Mincey was badly drunk and in danger of pissing off his audience, his rant was swerving perilously close to political, completely accidentally of course.

"Anyways, anyone shoots the facker, he gets a bottle of Jack Daniels and a Cowboys T shirt. Anyone stabs the cant he gets two bottles. Alright cowboys, let's ROCK!"

The band thundered into 'Rock'n'roll Fatwa'. Fortunately the song sounded exactly the same as all the other Leather Cowboys numbers, despite the ponderous subject matter.

Space Age Boogie baby, yeah!

Mincey had spotted Dandelion down at the front, man did she look hot! Bouncing them big fucking melons around all over the place, her gob looked like a big pink cunt, lovely, he could feel his purple pork trying to squeeze out of his leathers. Mincey pulled out all the stops, attempting stage moves that a man half his age would have had difficulty performing. When

Robbie saw him clambering onto the drum riser to do his flying splits the drummer felt his heart rise into his mouth. Mincey hadn't done this flying splits thing in over fifteen years! The last time was at a bikers' convention in Camber Sands, the poor bastard ended up in hospital after nearly losing his onions on one of the monitors.

Amazing even himself, the Mincer pulled it off, a perfect Dave Lee Roth flying splits thing. Mincey was driven by a megalithic sperm-shining lust to give the performance of his life, tongue flickering to obscene dimensions, buggery thrusting, microphone fellating, stage wanking, the man was fucking possessed.

Gerry Enchilada seemed to be picking up on Mincey's heat, slyly shagging his bass amp now and again, wiggling his builder's arse provocatively at a couple of pigs in lipstick down the front.

Dandelion was almost overcome by her orgasms, if she had any more she'd probably float away on them, they'd have to send air sea rescue to find her lost in a sea of fanny batter.

Sonny Darklord was vibing like no-one's business, an electric tornado of spasticised energy, banging out great sheets of sonic mayhem and pyrotechnical violence. Running around the stage like a madman with his cock hanging out, flopping all over the place, unbelievable.

A shadow at the back of The Fart and Chicken thought so too. Strutter Sandinista lurked by the bar nursing a can of Tennants Super, he was already having second thoughts about joining Peter Darklord's band The Tramps of Dawn. The man was an arsehole of monolithic proportions. He could be charm personified when he wanted something, but working with him for just over a month now, Strutter couldn't believe the transformation from urbane charmer into uncontrollable, rampant, megalomaniac tosspot. At least with Mincey he was always Mincey, this Darklord cunt was like Wurzel Gummidge, he had a different head on every fucking day. It was no surprise he paid such good wages, no one in their right mind would work with the bastard if he wasn't being paid a queen's ransom.

There was all that black magic shit as well, Darklord seemed to be trying to get Strutter to take part in some extremely dodgy sounding sex magick. Strutt didn't know exactly what it all meant but it appeared suspiciously shirtlifterish. He wasn't sure about the drummer Damien Warlock, but the bass player, Pink Starfish, was definitely of the bottomly persuasion.

Strutter could put up with Darklord's arseholishness for the 40 grand a week, but he drew the line at bumfoolery. Guinnivere could have the brat adopted before he started getting involved in any man-to-man boneriding or hornsmoking, no matter how many thousand quids he was being paid.

Strutter took a deep hit on his Tennents Super, weird, he could afford to drink champagne and single malts now but he still liked the thick treacly taste of the valerium laced, dosserjuice. He smiled and wiped his lips, Mincey was fucking good, you could keep your Jaggers and Tylers, Mincey was better, anyone who understood rock'n'roll, the elect grooviest of the groovy, knew it as well. If it hadn't been for the incident with the International Boss of the entire recording industry, Frankie Auschwitz and his transvestite son, who knows what heights they might have scaled? Or would they?

Rock'n'roll, real blistering, passionate rock'n'roll, always plays better on a diet of poverty and cheap drugs. Money and fame would have destroyed the Cowboys, transformed them overnight into another corporate, creamcheese, identiband. It was the lack of money and sometimes overbearing, torrential squalor that had bound them together all these years. His defection to The Tramps of Dawn for the Cosmosodomistic corporate dollar had proved that.

It's a simple fact that a band's first album is always their best - that precious handful of songs crafted on beat up guitars, cracked cymbals and broken amps.

Music shaped by a pure asceticism and a belief that the human spirit can conquer all.

Any form of success, no matter how close the band are initially, invariably ends up in distasteful, sad arguments about money and sordid, pointless nights in West End cocaine toilets.

Money, when passing through the pocket of the simple, instinctive creatures that are recording artists, is like a magnet to all the slimiest forms of life on the planet. Simply because said money is so easy to filch from the pockets of these naive and innocent dreamers.

Circling their prey like starving dogs, they line up for a pop at the pie. Stalking, avaricious, would-be wives, dolled up like pornographic orgasms. Insidious, homosexual, bad-breath managers. Flatulent, blowfly-posting, criminal promoters.

As for the feculent, festering record companies themselves, they should all be tried for child abuse and hung from the highest trees.

This, in a nutshell, is the ameliorating philosophy that the Cowboys had clung to all these unheated, shivering, cold water years. Why their creative star has never waned, why their last album 'Get Your Cock Out' was as startlingly brilliant as their first one, the classic 'Arsegrinder'.

Cosmic Space age boogie baby, yeah!

Chapter Twenty Two

Bill Drummond, Naked Excromancer

Bill Drummond, the internationally famous naked money burner, novelty rocker, polar explorer, adventurer, brown magician and Lightrary Arsehole strained hard on the chemical shitter. A few minutes later, having filled the entire bowl with about thirty pounds of steaming crap, he wiped his arse on a twenty pound note and took the whole stenching load up onto the deck of his houseboat. The converted long barge was moored in the most vile stretch of the Leeds and Liverpool canal he could find. It lurked in the damp shadows beneath a low railway bridge. The polluted, stagnant water was covered by a carpet of used condoms, pieces of broken styrofoam, crisp bags and plastic bottles. Stinking floating white belly-up perch, dead dogs and sacks of putrefying drowned kittens competed for attention in the disgusting necrotic menagerie. Hardly anyone used this stretch of the footpath behind the Shittersby Gasworks save the odd prowling paedophile and his 10 year old rat-boy prodigy frugging away in the suppurating, rank shadows.

This was the kind of solitude the idiosyncratic genius enjoyed. The brown magician, like a turdish Zarathustra, craved isolation far from the despicable blowflys of the market place. Only instead of the icy Carpathian mountains, the hermetic loner preferred the claustrophobic darkness of his railway bridge.

He poured the slopping contents of his chemical toilet onto the small deck at the back of the barge and lit a few candles. The stink was so bad it even made its odiferous presence felt through the miasmic fug of the sewerish canal. Hunching down next to the huge pile of loose stools the magician started using his hands to feel around in the massive pile of black shit. It appeared as if he was looking for something, up to the elbows in the stuff he was. He sniffed a handful here and there and eventually found the treasures he was looking for - four or five small black arse stones.

Bill was an excromancer, he could see into the future by reading the signs thrown up in his own excrement. His was a rare gift. More common practisers of the brown art needed the stools of the person whose fortune they were telling, but not the talented Scotsman, he could read other peoples' destiny by using his own turds.

Bill made a few magical gestures with some lifelike wooden carvings of turds and threw them in his pile. He shook the black arse stones in his hands like dice, blew on them three times and flung them into the crap. He performed a little shamanistic dance around his shit and then performed the farts of the four winds, lifting up his cak stained kilt and farting in a north, south, east and westerly direction. He was now ready to read his shit.

It was a difficult yet reliable craft, the consistency and position of the different subtle shades of brown, black, yellow and grey were all significant, as was the positioning of the arse stones and the wooden turds and the movements of the flies as they dined on their free faecal banquet. Bill studied hard for almost two hours. He was deeply concerned by what he had found. He absent-mindedly rubbed his shitty hand across his mouth and re-checked his notes.

He knew in his heart however that the turds never lie.

He pushed the huge pile of flyblown shit into the canal.

The cock rocker, Mincey Harris was in mortal danger, as was his new love Dandelion Dandelion. The brown magician hauled anchor on his longboat The Hysterical Bitch and set off at full speed for London. If he encountered no major difficulties and sailed through the night he might just make it in under a month. The Hysterical Bitch was a hardy vessel, its previous owner, Captain Arsebeard, had been a good sailor and had kept the Bitch shipshape for over fifty years.

Ever since accidentally meeting the singer around the back of The Rising Bunghole Sushi Bar in Tottenham Court Road the Scottish excromancer and private exorcist had been concerned about the man, he had the aura of someone about to be unjustly plagued by dark forces. Bill farted expansively and lit his pipe. The barge chugged its way into the Satanic blackness of the Yorkshire Pennines.

Chapter Twenty Three

The Transcendent Genius of Zodiac Mindwarp and The Aztecs of Sodom

Zodiac Mindwarp, the devastatingly handsome retired Rock God, lit a cigar and rang the bell for his butler. Still in his prime, the ridiculously intelligent chess grand-master waited patiently for his manservant. The debonair ultra-genius was dressed in a beautiful red and gold embroidered smoking jacket, a gift from his old flame, the Princess of Wales. Mindwarp had romanced almost all of the house of Windsor's beauties - including the strangely attractive Princess Anne herself.

The horsey Princess was particularly keen on taking it viciously up the khyber. Being one of nature's natural aristocrats, Zed enjoyed making love to fellow bluebloods. Their schooling in restraint and sexual perversion made sure that the women didn't die of sheer sexual ecstasy - an unfortunately common occurrence when the cosmic king of sex pleasured lesser-born mortals.

The dead movie star cooling in his four poster bed for instance.

The poor girl had orgasmed herself into extinction, her petit mort - "the little death" as those poetic lovers the French call it - being unfortunately more than just a tad petit this time.

The butler, Gimpo, entered the room. On seeing the dead woman sprawled naked across the bed, he commented drily "Another one sir, how many's that this week? Fifteen? Sixteen?""

"Good Lord man, no!" replied the dashing rocker. "She's the twenty third, old boy, or have you forgotten those Greek heiresses? Anyway, help yourself, the filly's still warm."

Gimpo undid his trousers carefully and without further ado buggered the attractive corpse vigorously, shouting into her deaf ears, calling her a whore, a bitch and a dead cunt.

"Really Gimpo, there's no need for such language," admonished the sexual athlete. "The poor thing can't hear you, She's like all the rest of them, death through orgasm, fucked to death. Oh well, when you've finished, place her in the mortuary and we'll send them all off to the superintendent at the end of the week".

Zodiac stood by the louvered windows of his beautiful stately home.

It was once owned by the Duke of something or other, until he lost it to Mindwarp in a game of poker. Everything that Zodiac did, he did it superbly and without compare and gambling for high stakes was no exception. The Duke's beautiful wife came with the house. The poor thing. She too, unable to withstand the juddering violence of multiple orgasms firing off like shooting stars, had died of unbearable sexual pleasure.

Gimpo's arse juddered spastically as he banged his cock snot deep into the dead girl's gut. The violence of his necrotic sodomy had torn the poor dead thing's sphincter along the perineum, creating one large black hole between her legs. He pulled his shitty dick out of her mangled jacksie/cunt and wiped it on her hair before throwing the exquisite corpse over his shoulder. A brown watery fluid trickled from the dead girl's hugely dilated and torn anus, down the back of her legs, mixing with the thick black blood from the ruptured perineum.

The aesthete Mindwarp pulled a face, obviously suffering acute nausea at the poor young girl's ringly condition.

"It's funny how death does that to them" he remarked to himself, turning away and gazing forlornly across the vast acres. The rolling hills had been elegantly landscaped during the 17th century by the master gardener Capability Brown. Zode poured himself a glass of finest breakfast champagne and sat at his work desk to compose a few lines of poetry.

"The American woman was on the telephone again,

sir," said Gimpo standing in the doorway with the dead girl dripping spermy bean juice onto the priceless Persian carpets.

"Oh God, not again! When will the talentless slut let it go? You'd think that now her cabbage had been turned inside out by little Lourdes and her paps shrivelled up into lactatating paper bags she'd lay off all this soft focus sex rubbish. Good lord, how old is the demented woman? She's at least forty. The woman's a crone for God's sake!" said the genius.

"She's offering money as well now, sir" said the butler, sticking a tissue up the corpse's dripping buggery-socket. "Twenty million, just to fellate you, sir," he carried on, wiping her shitty leg.

"Good Lord, doesn't the silly cow know I'm doing her a favour? She obviously has no idea how many women have died of orgasmic overdose by simply chowing down on the Mindwarp gristle-hammer!"

Distracted by the American singer's constant harrasment the man of genius flung down his pen and amused himself by perusing some of his beautifully bound first editions. The learned and sophisticated star had one of the finest private libraries in the world. It was acquired during another lucky night at the tables. The Earl of Buggersford, poor chap, killed himself after losing everything. His beautiful young wife, as often happens in these situations, flung herself at the unrivalled king of sensuality and amazingly brilliant sex.

"Any more messages Gimps?" asked Zodiac, crossing his legs and peering over his gold rimmed reading glasses.

"Just the usual Society strumpets, sir. American film stars, Greek shipping heiresses and the like", replied the Butler. "Oh and your friend, the flatulent chap, what's his name?"

"Billy! Billy Drummond! I say!" laughed the manly singer. "My God, I haven't seen old rat-up-his-arse Billy boy since we snowboarded down the north face of the Eiger together last Christmas! Did he say what it was he wanted? I wonder what that cracked old moneyburning rascal is up to these days!" mused the handsome adventurer. "The last I heard he was holed up with some Indian Rishi learning all about Excromancy. Buggering around with his operatic arsehole, predicting the apocalypse by the lay of his turds. Good old Billy! He's a one!"

The singer's spirits were plainly lifted. Despite the terrible flatulence of his friend, the two maverick and visionary geniuses had much in common. Obviously Zodiac was way and above and by far the better looking of the two, his penis being a good eight inches longer and much, much fatter than the Scotsman's. But in spite of this disadvantage, the Brown Magician was no slouch at all when it came to the ladies.

Despite or perhaps even because of his gibbering taste for extremely frightening and violently perverted, shit-slinging, buggery and torture-sex, women were irresistably drawn to the arse- blasting Jock's violent and miasmic charisma.

The butler informed his master that Mr Drummond would be arriving in a few hours by narrowboat (the Leeds and Liverpool canal traversed the Mindwarp estate in the far north-eastern corner).

"Saddle up Demon would you, Gimpo? I think I'll meet the old bugger by the canal," said the superb horseman, pulling on his black riding boots. "And turn out the men, I don't think Billy's seen my private guard yet." The supersonic judo expert was referring to the forty crack biker commandoes, The Aztecs of Sodom MC.

This heavily armed cadre of humongous tattooed giants were cherry picked from the most ferocious outlaw motorcycle gangs in the world. Zed was the President. His Vice President, Jesus Con Carne was the former leader of the notorious Mexican Outlaw bikers Les Fuckeros, stone killers to the man.

This gang of monstrously violent yet extremely disciplined bike warriors were made up almost exclusively of French foreign legion veterans.

Jesus, after Zodiac himself, was probably one of the hardest men alive. He had sworn allegiance to the Mindwarp colours after Zodiac had defeated him in savage and brutal armed combat. Zodiac gave the brave biker warrior quarter after pinning him to the floor and cutting the biker's face with his razor sharp Bali Song knife to let him know that, if he had wanted, he could have killed the Mexican brute easily. The biker now carried the livid scar across his left cheek as a badge of honour.

Somewhere in the maze of ultra-masculinity and bubbling, testosteronic machismo, the psychology of this terrifying troop of two wheeled warriors had bent sinister and the men had sworn a weird oath of homosexuality - a terrifying violent strain of inversion, more Ronnie Kray than Julian Clarey. No one was quite sure how all this had happened, the Aztecs' contempt for spiritual and physical weakness and anything remotely feminine probably went some way to explaining this strange sphincterial situation. They found, however, that their brand of sadistic homosexuality struck mortal terror into the hearts of the enemy. Anyone crossing either Z or his Aztecs knew that not only would they be savagely beaten to bloody hamburger but they would also suffer horrific and dreadful arse torture.

Z mounted his beautiful jet black Arab stallion, its massive pink tube-steak swinging arrogantly below its belly, and, accompanied by his loyal biker warriors, set off across the rolling landscape of his own personal stretch of Yorkshire land.

His fellow adventurer, the money-burning fartist and brown magician Bill Drummond, was working his strange faecal sorcery in the tiny galley of The Hysterical Bitch when he heard the approach, like low flying WW2 aircraft, of Z and his fearsome Aztecs of Sodom.

He rattled off a nervous one and peered out of a porthole. A cloud of fartdust and noise appeared on the horizon, gradually approaching the canal, a man on horseback at their lead. He recognised the regal bearing of his friend Zodiac and stepped onto the deck of his rickety narrow boat, smiling at the bombastic glamour of the man. The four-eyed Scotch geggy pumped loudly and pushed his dirty glasses up his nose. He had some serious news for his kingly friend.

Back in the drawing room of his beautiful home, Zodiac was less than pleased when his brown Magician friend lifted up his kilt and unloaded about twenty pounds of horrendous smelling shit in front of the open log fire. It was a miracle where the Excromancer kept it all. The retired rock God raised his hand as one of the Aztecs of Sodom, Hernadez 'Big Davy' Cocksockett - a Mexican/French-Canadian Vietnam veteran - pulled out a huge Bowie Knife and almost threw it at the dumping Ipissimus Magus.

"Cool it Davy, it's sorcery. Fucking stinking sorcery but magic all the same."

Covering his face with a scented handkerchief, Z listened patiently as Bill explained the lay of his shite. The brown magician wasn't entirely certain as to the exact meaning of his recent shittings but it was serious and it involved one of Zodiac's old friends, Mincey Harris and that perverter of the craft, Peter Darklord. Nether Bill nor Zed had any time for the pretentious front man with the pompous outfit The Tramps of Dawn. He was a dreadful singer and a bad magician. His craft was black. Which, in the dangerous worlds of sorcery, meant that the man's magic was being used for selfish egotistical ends instead of the altruistic goals of a master magician.

The hidden forces of the universe are neutral. A master of the craft must be beyond such pithy human constructs as good or evil.

The Manichaean concept of duality was the reason for mankind's metaphorical banishment from Eden, from its loss of innocence and the pure grace of animals. Mankind's actions, bound by this flawed construct has been more or less the single cause of all preventable suffering for the past two thousand years and beyond. German soldiers in World War Two had the words "Gott mit uns" - God be with us - embossed on their belt buckles. There is a famous story from the battlefront of an American soldier coming across this phrase on a fallen foe's belt. The teenage warrior was distraught beyond reassurance. The poor lad was under the impression that God was on Uncle Sam's side.

    Bill shovelled the steaming pile into the fire.
    And cleared the room.

Chapter Twenty Four

Genuine Downs Syndrome Beauty
44 48 56
all services

Peter Darklord would have been unrecognisable to even his biggest fan. The black-magician's fingers trembled as he dialled the numbers for the mongol prostitute.

As George Michael's amusing run-in with the LAPD illustrates, even the sanctuary of great wealth cannot shield its owners from the bizarre dictates of desire - witnss Georgey Porgey's throbbing libido taking control of the powerless superstar's will and commanding the famous shirtlifter to surreptitiously wank himself off into a policeman's pocket.

Similar yet far worse demons were working on the perverse Peter Darklord. Ever since his childhood the mysterious front man had had a thing about those enchanted subnormals, Mongoloid's. His very first sexual encounter ever had been in a barn at his uncles farm with Fat Betty, his downs syndrome cousin. Although considerably older than the eleven year old Peter, mentally she was about 7 or 8 years old and, like a lot of Downys, the salacious mong was sex-mad. The image of strapping Betty slurping down on the junior magician's pre-pubescent wood was still the main fantasy feature in the grown man's fevered tug-frenzies.

As a magician Darklord was proud of his self control. It was only during periods of intense anxiety that the irrepressible urge to fuck a mong's fat arse sideways took possession of him. This trembling loss of self control had hit him like shit from a busted fan when he heard that his son and only heir, Sonny Darklord, was playing lead guitar with the Leather Cowboys. The fact that the vacancy was created by his underhand procurement of Strutter Sandanista for The Tramps of Dawn only underlined this feeling of lack of self control.

"Hello," said the voice on the other end of the line, an old voice. An ex brass herself no doubt, cunt and desirability nowway too wretched even for the most depraved libertine.

"It's about the advert in the phone box.." said Peter, guilt already chewing him up inside. He was an internationally famous rock star, what the fuck was all this shit about?!

"Yes sir, would you like some details?" continued the old hag, her voice sounded like nicotine, phlegm and old cats' tongues, her false teeth whistled down the line, revolting the cultured Magician as he squirmed within the oily jail of his shameful weakness. Why couldn't he be into schoolgirl-spanking? Or bondage, enemas, watersports, fisting - anything! Anything other than this embarrassing sub-shafting business!

"Yes p-p-please..." Darklord stammered like a choirboy during the dreaded ball dropping months of puberty.

"Well she's a beautiful downs syndrome girl sir, her features are very pronounced, like a little Elf she is sir. She's 21 years old with a mental age of about seven, a lovely cuddly 44 48 56 figure. She provides a full service, sir and her fees start at £30. A full personal service is £85, would you like the address sir?" chirruped the old slapper.

"H-H-How much is it for the sodomy, please?" asked Peter. He could feel a bead of sweat trickling between his buttocks and collecting in his palpitating sphinc.

"Would that be on yourself sir? Or would you yourself be wanting to bugger the young lady?" retorted Mama Pervoid, a twinkle of cruel humour in her phlegmy delivery

"Buggering the mong of course." said Peter, all indignant. God, bumming subnormals was bad enough, being shafted by a mongoloid whorebag pumping a strap-on Donkey Kong Intruder up his starfush didn't even bare thinking about!

Peter made his way along Wardour street and ducked up Meard street, past Gossips night club and into the small back ginnels around Northern Soho till he found the address. A red light shone in the first floor window. His boner was straining inside his sweaty silk underpants in anticipation as he climbed the narrow ricketty stairs.

The crone answered the door, he recognised her congealed voice as she led him into the meanly furnished flat.

"Delilah's busy at the moment sir, so if you'd like to wait in here...". Peter entered the grim room and sat on the creaky bed. The threadbare curtains were closed, a single bare lightbulb threw a weak 40 watts of electric light onto his theatre of degradation. The old maid entered the room without knocking and switched on the old dirt stained portable colour TV and turned on a video.

"She won't be long sir, she's with another client, you can watch some naughty films to get you in the mood..". She left the room leaving the faint aroma of her profession - johnnys, spunk, baby oil and KY jelly. The film flickered into visibility. It was obviously home-made. A fat old grey-pubed man wearing a leather mask was getting noshed by a fat mongol. That must be Delilah he thought. She wasn't bad if you got rid of the stupid tart costume of purple rayon bra, cheap stockings and suspenders, God only knows what the man's string Y fronts were all about but it seemed to be working for old papa grey bollocks. The randy pensioner was unloading his pud water all over the smiling mentaloid's face. The movie juddered a little, a blizzard of static jumped in and faded and there was the game mong riding some shiny tube of dog cock, a big fucking alsation. The freak seemed to be enjoying herself, laughing as the over-excited German Sheperd kept slipping out of her meaty cabbage. There was another fast cut to the sexy pixie sat on the toilet with a mischievous look on her face. Peter quickly turned the TV off, he was in danger of shooting his load before Delilah had even entered the room.

The cheerful sub walked in smiling, a silk black

nightie covering her ample frame. My God but she was a big fucker! She bounced down next to Peter, almost breaking the bed, her smile was like sunshine.

"Ith it the bumming you want?" she said cheerily, She sounded like Jack Ashley MP. The poor thing was obviously hard of hearing. Peter nodded "Leth have a look then" she said, tugging at his pants like an excited child pulling at an Xmas present. Peter's spindly old man poked out of his pants, it was thin and pointed. Delilah laughed with delight and threw off her black nightie.

She had on a pair of white boxer shorts and a yellow flowery bra. The enthusiastic lass bent over the bed. "Go on then mithter, thtick it in" she said cheerfully over her shoulder. The maid entered with a little tube of KY and an industrial strength condom.

"If you don't mind sir? As you can see Delilah is very enthusiastic. It's for your own sake as well as hers..". She left the buggery lotion and Durex on the little table at the side of the bed. The magician was so lost in desire he didn't bother with either and rammed his gristle up to the conkers in Delilah's big fat arse. His knees gave way beneath him as he banged off almost the second he was locked in the mongy's wet velvet shitlocker. Delilah giggled happily and did a little wriggle to dislodge the magician's deflating pork.

"Thank you, bye bye" she smiled, her beautiful almond shaped eyes magnified behind jam jar bottomed national health style specs.

Peter zipped up his pants with trembling hands. Feelings of shame and horror, anger and fear assailed him before the blood had even drained from his prick. He hurtled down the rickety stairs and out into the night, his flies weren't even buttoned. He tucked his shirt in angrily as he walked quickly down Berwick Street. He had to try and make amends to his son.

This perversion shit was getting out of hand. How could he bugger his own son, just because the tabloids had

been ranting on about paedophiles.
   What did he think he was missing!?

Chapter Twenty Five

Rubber Bitch Lesbian Cock fight

Mincey Harris was experiencing intimate rapture with Dandelion Dandelion, their souls falling through the universe like petals from a cascading cosmic flower.

"Oh Mincey!" she breathed in his ear.

"Dandelion Dandelion!" he replied.

Their passionate lovemaking had elevated them far above the Fart and Chicken's small blocked-up khazi. Their souls were united with the universe, for theirs was a love divine.

"Hey Meencey, hurry the fock up, maan, I need to do the sheet man...."

It was the fat Mexican bass player Gerry Enchilada. His crude interruption pulled them down from heaven as fast as a surprise attack of chronic diarrhoea. This frantic coupling was what had driven them apart the last time. Losing themselves in blocked toilets, that fucking floater...

"Mincey please!" said Dandelion, taking her mouth away from his for a second. "Somewhere else, not here, here in the toilet, with the smell of shit and industrial strength cocaine."

She needn't have worried, Mincey had taken the liberty of booking a room at The Spermly Waves Hotel - an exotic lovers' hideaway in Notting hill.

It was owned and run by a hopelessly romantic, '70s songbird, Anouska De Paul. The big-eyed babe was an expert at cosmetic preservation just this side of the knife and was still vaguely fuckable. Her head, as was obvious from the baroque fantasies invoked by the unique rooms, was stuffed with Art Noveau, romantic, pot pourri nonsense.

Mincey had slipped her several portions of spam over the years. The singer liked her, she was cool about his smack and was partial to the odd gouch-out session herself.

Mincey and Dandelion fell into the back of the black cab, tongue-wrestling and feeling each other's genitals through their clothes.

Arse Johnson, the cabdriver had never seen anything like it. He'd witnessed the odd blow job, usually drunk slappers, and he didn't mind as long as the slags didn't throw up when the baby gravy slimed their epiglottis. He remembered one of the girls from Cockarama, the girly singing group, blowing chunks all down the bass player from goth horror band Dead Funny's leather strides. But these two? She had her arse in the air and her pervert boyfriend, after jacking up in his eyeball, had started sucking on her bumhole through the knickers as if his life depended on it. The girl couldn't have been more than 16 and there she was with this filthy drug monkey, hoovering his pink trumpet like a woman twice her age. Poor Arse, he nearly crashed the cab a couple of times, wanking away furiously in the front whilst steering erratically with one hand.

Anouska was delighted when Mincey had called to book a room for himself and his new girlfriend. Being partial to cunt-sucking as well as hetero-buggery the bisexual hotelier assumed Mincey would invite her to join in with the the action. She hoped he had some heroin as well, there was nothing better for post copulatory relaxation than a fat line of skag. The '70s dolly bird trowelled on another layer of slap, if it weren't for the slight lines around her big cocksucking lips she could easily pass for 17, or so she thought.

The door bell rang, it was Mincey and the girl.

"Darling, you look wonderful!" said Anouska, kissing him dramatically on the cheek

"And whose this beautiful little thing?" she said, sizing up Dandelion Dandelion. She couldn't wait to get down on the youngster's fresh clam.

Peter introduced Dandy and excused the pair of them

while they went up to their room. Anouska would join them later, letting him get a few rounds off first so he could take his time with the lusty bisexual.

As soon as the door to their incredibly overdone room, pot pourri and velvet drapes fucking everywhere - was closed, Mincey started stabbing away, giving the breathless girl a serious titfucking.

"Oh Mincey!" she breathed as the horse-cocked singer banged away between her formidable knockers. She was kneeling on the floor, holding them tightly together as her man shifted north from mammary valley and started fucking her face. Dandy nearly choked, her Dad hadn't taught her the deep throat technique that most of the Mincer's slags were capable of. She pulled his straining spunkbone from her mouth.

"Not so fast darling, I want to savour your body like wine". Dandy didn't know where the fuck that little piece of shit poetry had come from, probably one of her mothers bodice rippers. Then she carried on blowing Mincey's cheesy horn.

They went at it for two hours solid. Dandy was experiencing her fortyfifth orgasm when Mincey farted loudly and came out of the bathroom. She spat Arse Johnson's cock out of her mouth and looked down at her cunt where Anouska was licking away like a sly cat.

"What the fuck! Mincey!" she shouted as the wanking cabby spurted his pud juice all over the 16 year old's monster mams. The hotelier took her mouth off the youngsters dripping clam jungle and started laughing as the distraught teenager cried "Mincey ! What's going on?"

Dandy was furious. She couldn't understand how she hadnt noticed these two old perverts feeding on her, they were like vampires, especially that old bitch between her legs. And the cabbie, God - he was disgusting! He'd just spurted his watery jizz all over her tits and was still mashing away, a huge rubber cock stuffed up his arse like a tail.

Mincey looked confused. To the debauched singer this was all perfectly normal. The old bag started laughing.

"Don't say your little princess is a virgin, Mincey?!" she mocked. The cabbie was still mashing away and had managed to squirt out another splash of vinegar which caught Dandy in the eye. This was all going terribly wrong, first the fucking floater, now all this group sex weirdness, the poor thing broke down in tears. Anouska started laughing cruelly. Big mistake. Dandy yanked the rubber cock out of Arse Johnson's jacksie and started battering the mocking slag around the head with it.

"I'll show you whose a fucking virgin, you lesbian bitch!" Anouska's laughter had been replaced by screams, the girl was strong, the rubber cock heavy.

The bisexual felt her nose break, blood spurted all over the beautiful silk sheets. Dandy brought the shit-stained dildo down again and again, breaking Anouska's cheek bones and jaw. Arse Johnson was bashing away even faster - this was better than porno! A real bitch fight! The wanker grabbed another three foot gentleman's dildo from a creepy looking rubber Gladstone bag and rammed it hard up his baggy sphinc, another jet of vinegar spurted across the room. Arse was having the time of his life!

"Please! No Mistress!" he said, struggling into a rubber mask and dropping to his knees. Dandy smacked the meta-perv full in the face with the bloody cock, smashing Arse's dentures into pieces, the man could feel them floating around inside the rubber hood amongst all the blood. Then she floored the wanking cabbie with a brutal karate kick to the balls. Anouska was gurgling on the floor, a growing pool of blood soaking into the elaborate Persian carpet. It would take a fucking good plastic surgeon to fix the shattered rubble that was all that was left of the vain woman's face. Dandy flung the bloody, shit stained cock onto the floor.

"What's your fucking problem. Harris!?" she shouted at the dumbstruck singer.

"My problem, you crazy facking bitch!?" he shouted back. "Look what you've done to Nouskha!" he said, pointing at the seriously splattered woman choking on her own blood. Arse had started weakly wanking again while curled up in a foetal ball on the floor.

"Oh Mincey!" simpered Dandelion, falling into the singer's arms. "Our first lovers' tiff!". Mincey smiled and ran his fingers through her long dark hair.

"Look at that cunt!" he laughed, pointing at the tugging taxi driver on the floor. "He facking loves it!"

Anouska, despite the pain of her shattered face was also secretly pleased. This was the perfect excuse to have a new face made for herself. Bardot's lips she thought, Liz Taylor's nose, oh joy indeed. And Diana Ross's eyes!

Mincey called an ambulance and the two lovers fled into their desperado night, fondling each other's genitals in the back of another cab. The GBH had brought them even closer together. Dandelion swallowed her lover's thick sperm as they pulled up outside the singer's squalid flat. The cabbie waived the young lovers' fare, smiling fondly as he told them that he'd had the best wank of his life while watching the two of them rutting away in his rear-view mirror. Bumhole through the knickers and everything! Fantastic.

Off he tugged, into the rain, beeping his horn and smiling happily as he twanged his cockney monkey spanner.

The two lovers buggered, fellated, fucked, wanked and muffdived till the dawn's early light slid through the holes in Mincey's filthy curtains. Mincey watched his precious Dandelion as she slept and smiled lovingly at the silvery, flaky sperm stains on her face and hair.

Then he decided to wake her with a gentle fuck up her arsehole.

Chapter Twenty Six

Bumfucker Blues

Strutter Sandinista was seriously regretting joining The Tramps of Dawn. The whole bunch of them were full-on arsebandits of salamiastic proportions. If Pink Starfish made one more camp little joke at the extremely heterosexual Strutter's expense then he was going to find out what a Gibson Explorer felt like jammed up his pink fucking starfish arse, the spunkbone-jockey faggot.

And, as if the constant teasing by the band of fucking fairies wasn't enough, the ridiculous salary he was receiving from Darklord had completely gone to his partner Guinnevere's head. Guinnevere wasn't her real name, obviously, Guinnevere Ladysmith? Fuck right off! Her real name was Meg Cider and she was from the Wyther estate in the Stanningley district of Leeds.

The money had changed the thick bitch completely. She was spending Strutter's moolah faster than he was earning it. Never a classical beauty, the fat pig was blowing thousands on shitty Sloane street designer crap. Haut Couture that only looked good on skinny drag Queens, not rock chicks well past their big-arsed sell by dates. More than one flustered bumboy designer had banned her from his shops, no amount of money was worth seeing their beautiful creations made to look like the polyester pant suits as favoured by overweight, middle aged American housewives.

Sitting in the middle of Strutter's dilapidated council flat in her travesty of Azzedina Alia, sipping Bollinger from a pint pot, flipping through a load of estate agent bollocks, the fashion disaster continued her brainless twittering .

"Hampstead's nice, but Chelsea's got nicer shops. What do you think, Strutter? Why don't you get some Versace Strutter darling? He does some lovely rock things for Elton and Mick."

What the fuck was wrong with her? She was talking as if Elton and Mick were friends of theirs. Strutter loathed those rich old cunts. Why would he want to wear the same spangly Liberace dogshit those poofters draped themselves in? He cracked open another purple tin. He'd already seen off five and it wasn't even noon yet. Guinnevere, Meg Cider, was on her second or third bottle of Bollinger, Strutter was sure she wasn't supposed to be caning it in her condition, the cunt was four months fucking pregnant.

"Oh champagne's not like lager, the doctor said it was good for the baby," the fat bitch lied.

The white stretch limo pulled up outside the front door, Guinnevere kissed Strutter on both cheeks, that was new as well, as was calling him darling all the time - the fat cunt was turning into Magenta Divine, darling. The disgruntled Strutter crushed the purple tin in his fist and threw it at the knackered gas fire, popping another Tennents Super almost immediately.

Strutter put on a CD, wiping a tear away as 'Bumfucker' from them early Cowboy's album 'Kingly Salami' blasted out of the speakers.

"Bumfucker, Bumfucker, Bumfucker, yes I am, oh yeah!" went the catchy chorus. It was the early '70's - glam rock and rampant arsebanditry were fashionable back then.

"Bumfucker Bumfucker Bumfucker, oh yeah! I'm gonna fuck you baby till your liver falls out! Oh yeah, come on and bumfuck me Strutter, alright! Woo!" sang Mincey, camper than a boy scout jamboree, before Strutt's mental guitar solo came screaming in like a German Stuka divebomber. Strutter smiled, he could remember recording 'Bumfucker' in some funky little studio underneath a pizza joint in Coptic Street near the British Museum.

Strutter sat down on his old armchair, the small council flat was stuffed with piles of designer clothes, some of them worn for ten minutes and then discarded. As for the shoes, Imelda fucking Marcos had nothing on Guinnevere Meg Cider fucking Ladysmith. Strutter threw back the sickly dregs of his purple tin and had a wank, jizzing all over the estate agent crap his bitch had shovelled in the door.

"Bumfucker bumfucker bumfucker yeah alright!" screamed Mincey. Strutter burst into tears, what the fuck had he done!

The depressed guitarist picked up his Gibson Explorer and started riffing through some of his favourite Cowboys tunes - 'Lesbian Tamer', 'Cockfighting Man', and 'Cannonballs'.

Each song brought back different memories, they were like aural snapshots. 'Lesbian Tamer' was written about Gerry Enchilada's conviction that any woman who wouldn't suck on his spicy pork roll seconds after meeting him was a lesbian.

'Cockfighting Man' reminded him of the time the big Mexican had burnt the studio down during the recording of the song. The clumsy beaner's midnight feast of refried beans and tacos came to an explosive end after the fat chef had left the gas oven on.

'Cannonballs' more or less spoke for itself. A great wave of melancholia swept over him as he realised that he would never rock on the same stage as his loyal and closest friends ever again.

Twenty five years they'd been rocking. Against all the odds. Just the four of them, against the world. Frankie Auschwitz and all his Cosmosodomistic dark forces couldn't stop them. And now? The stupid idiot had sold his soul for what? He picked up some of Guinnevere's coutre shit- a stupid looking dress covered in acres of third world embroidery. For this!? He tore the piece of rubbish in two. He started on the rest, ripping them up and slinging them out of the window, the Tennents had stoked his rage right through the responsibility barrier. The demented guitarist started piling all the shoes, the handbags, fucking Prada! All the stupid dresses and estate agent lies into a huge pile in the middle of the room. After pouring lighter fuel all over Guinnevere fucking Meg Fucking bitch stupid slag fucking Cider's ridiculous shit he was about to torch his little bonfire of vanities when the phone rang.

"Who the fack is it!?"

. Strutter listened a few seconds then put down the phone. His eyes filled with tears, he started smiling and then punched the air.

"Yes!" he shouted. "Rock and fackin' roll, baby!" He turned up the CD and sang along to the glorious racket belching out of the speakers.

"Bumfucker! Bumfucker! Bumfucker! Alright!"

He squealed off into an air guitar solo, miming to his own music.

Guinnevere - Meg Cider- had just lost the baby. The fat drunken cow had dropped the bloody mess in the changing rooms of some poncey New Bond Street fashion coutre bollock joint.

Apparently she'd guzzled down two bottles of Bollinger in the shop and, after trying on nearly every dress in the place and buying all of them. had started haemorrhaging big time, blood and jelly splattering all over the five-grand mini skirts, the assistants were in a tiz, this had never happened before, the stock was being ruined.

The foetus itself slurped out of Meg's distended cabbage and onto the floor, her back end had gone as well and a great barrage of champagne shit blurted out onto the fully developed foetus wriggling around like something out of Ridley Scott's Alien. The drunken Meg screamed and passed out, falling into the aborted gore, waving her credit cards and screaming for more champagne.

On hearing the good news, Strutter cracked open his seventh can of purple liver stench and set off to Nomis rehearsal rooms to do his "I quit"! number. Pink fucking Starfish indeed.

The guitarist was very drunk.

Pink Starfish was riding Damien Warlock's cocksockett violently when Strutter kicked open the rehearsal room door.

"Ooh we've got guests, Pinky!" said the depraved drummer. Pink was lost in brown lust and didn't hear his special friend, he was just about to let loose his vinegar.

Strutter said nothing and grabbed hold of Pink's Fender precision bass by the neck. He walked across to the bumming rhythm section and whacked the buggerist Starfish full in the face. Pink screamed as he popped out of the drummer's arse and fell backward showering his bumchum with broken teeth and blood. Damien Warlock started screaming like a girl, Strutter kicked the drummer in the face, breaking his jaw and cheekbone.

The drummer tried to pull his pants up but Strutter kneed him in his face and whacked him sparko with a killer rabbit punch. Strutt leapt over the kit and grabbed hold of Starfish by his peroxide bouffant. The bass player was screaming through his ruined mouth. Then Strutter started banging the arse-rocker's head against the floor. He didn't stop till the bass player's face was hamburger, every tooth in his cocksucking mouth smashed on the stone floor.

The guitarist dipped his finger in the great lake of blood leaking from Starfish's face and wrote I QUIT in the bassist's gore all over the back wall of the rehearsal room wall. The fact that the Cowboys might not want the guitarist back in the band never occurred to him. His self loathing for his shitty behaviour was still raging in his Tennants stoked brain. Shaking with rage and alcohol, he broke the neck off the Fender precision bass and, after pulling Pink's pink leather strides around his ankles, rammed the neck of the guitar up Starfish's starfish - right up to the lungs. The guitarist laughed at the gruesome tableau he'd created and set off for Fat Arsed Frank's sleazy rehearsal rooms on the other side of town, Kings Cross.

Rock on baby, yeah!

Chapter Twenty Seven

Croaked Jizzmuncher

Sonny Darklord was on the spit. Gerry Enchilada had bagsied the jacksie and was thrusting hard up the kid's chufter chute. Robbierre Le Vomiteur was fucking pretty boy's face. Mincey was shivering in the corner of the damp, filthy rehearsal room, the poor bastard was doing his cold turkey. Now that he had Dandelion he was trying to clean up his act. This time his determination had lasted fourteen hours, one more time he said pulling up his eyelid and jabbing the needle underneath his left eyeball.

Fuck it, he reasoned I might as well do it properly, get some methadone.

"What's facking happened?" said Robierre as Sonny's body went slack.

"Hey, maan, shut up your mouth, maan, I'm coming up on my vineegar stroke man, uuugh!"

The Fat Mexican, his bootcut jeans around his knees, snapped off an ugly wad into the kid's lower intestine. Once he released the skinny teenager the floppy body fell to the ground, blood leaking from the nose. The poor bastard was dead, he'd choked on Robbie's dick. The smack Mincey had given him was primo stuff, twice the strength of the usual brown that floated around Kings Cross. He had been in no condition to be blowing anyone, let alone be on the spit, his choke reaction had been nullified by the heroin and he'd suffocated on the drummer's deep throating wood. Grim.

The two part time bummers didn't even notice. They started banging around on the drums and bass, searching for kick-ass riffs, they seemed to find one, a mean growling thing it was. So lost in their groove they didn't notice as Strutt wandered into the room, plugged his Explorer into the dead kid's amp and added his savage fretwork.

The riff exploded, Robb smashed the cymbals as Gerry started pumping the beat, Mincey grabbed the mike and was just about to start singing when he clocked Strutter on guitar.

Nothing seemed strange at first, so used was Mince to singing with his best buddy wanging away beside him

"Fack, man!" he gasped into the mike. "Gerry, Robbie, pack it in, man! Look who's here! Little Lord Judas himself!".

If the cocky bastard thought he could just wander into the rehearsal rooms like nothing had happened then he could facking think again. Although Sonny was a fantastic player, he would never achieve the streamlined insanity of Strutter Sandinista - even Sonny himself had known that - but, fuck it, even if Strutter did want his old job back the facking cant was going to have to suffer some major humiliation first!

The big dumb old Tex Mex ran up to Strutter and gave him a big bear hug. He still had his cock out, it was covered in Sonny's shit.

"Fack off you dirty cant, what's that on your cock, you're facking disgusting, man!" laughed Strutter.

Mincey forgot about the planned humiliation of the prodigal plankspanker and ran up to his old buddy and embraced him.

"You facking bastard!" he choked, tears in his eyes. In many ways being in a band is like being in some weird fourway dysfunctional marriage - love, hate and all shades of infuriatingness inbetween. Mince was just glad to have the fucker back. It was Robbie who noticed the dead Sonny sparko on the floor. The poor dead fucker was bleeding from both ends.

"Shit," he said quietly, knowing the lad had croaked.

"Well, you know there's like a good side to everything," said Mincey when they'd all checked the dead guitarist. "We don't have to sack the facker!"

They all laughed. It was a good joke.

Mincey's attitude was not as callous as it might appear.

Rock casualties were common. Any fucker that lives life as free and loose as rock'n'rollers know that the grim reaper is only one stab away of too much bad fun. It's an unspoken thing but most of them would rather meet the big guy riding a glamorous OD, or some groovy bullet game gone wrong, a mad chick with a knife, anything really, as long as it was deliciously sordid and sleazy. It was a sure fire way of immortality. You stayed young forever, photographs of you looking sad and old, with dyed hair, grey hair, no hair or fake hair never appeared. Hair loss is the worse thing that can happen to a rock'n'roller. A glorious burn out, a car crash, an aeroplane crash, or a more literary gesture like Ernest Hemmingway and closet redneck Kurt Cobain with their funky little shotguns - all of these fast exits were far more preferable than the sad ignoble fates of the Mick Jaggers of the world, still chasing teenagers at 75 or however old the disgusting geriatric fucker was.

Of course, Mincey was 45 but, through some elaborate form of self deception, he didn't seem to realise this, the chump still thought he was 18.

Gerry checked the kid's pulse.

"He gone, maan! The little girlyboy ain't gonna smoke no more horn, that's for sure!" said the hirstute beaner with a tinge of regret. "Shit, he was a tasty piece of ass, maan, you flip him on his belly man, he was jus like a girl, maan, focker!"

Everyone assumed it was the heroin, which was kind of true. Even if Robbie hadn't have his ginormous beef-bayonet rammed savagely down the little buggerbandit's throat, he would have probably croaked anyway. Mincey and Strutter stuffed the already stiffening cadaver behind the amps, blue corpses gave Mincey the creeps (as you can imagine). Fat Frank's Rehearsal Room charged six pounds an hour, Sonny wasn't going anywhere. They'd call the ambulance when they'd finished rehearsing.

Chapter Twenty Eight

The Order Of The All Seeing Brown Eye

Peter Darklord, despite all the ringpiece abuse he'd dished out to his young son, still loved the boy. The usual adolescent tantrums and disobedience had obviously been complicated even further by all the buggery, even if it was in order to steel him for his eventual admittance to the black magical group his father had established - The Order Of The All Seeing Brown Eye.

The group was formed in the erly '70s by Peter and his two fellow masters of the Black Arts - Adam Ringworthy and the notorious German necromancer, Anus Deus. Total anal obedience was required of all acolytes. The order believed that the power of buggery-magic was one of the most ancient and efficient means of harnessing the invisible forces of nature and bending them to an individual's will. Darklord believed many famous men had been practitioners of Arse Magick. Adolf Hitler, Winston Churchill, Karl Marx, Freud. Some Arsists believed that Christ himself was a practitioner of the anal black arts. It was practiced extensively by the rabbis and Jewish cabballa magicians of the time he claimed, and they could have schooled the young Nazarene in the ways of the arse during those unaccounted for years in the desert.

Full initiation to The Order Of The Brown Eye began on an acolyte's 16th birthday. Peter had started his son's introduction to the powers of Sodom very early, hoping that one day the lad would become one of the greatest arse sorcerers the world had ever seen. Obviously the young man thought his father was completely insane and went to live with his mother,

Shirley Darklord, as soon as possible.

When the police informed Peter of his son's tragic death -an unsolved riddle involving serious sodomatic practices and heroin, Peter knew instinctively that those depraved animals, The Leather Cowboys, had something to do with it. His grief at losing his young son while simultaneously losing the services of his now traumatised and hospitalised rhythm section imploded dangerously in the mad magician's utterly corrupted mind.

To explain fully why Peter Darklord decided to avenge himself on singer Mincey Harris would be as difficult as trying to explain why Mark Chapman decided to kill John Lennon. Death was not revenge enough for the arse magician however, he knew that there were things far worse than death. Peter Darklord, through all the power of his diabolical dirtbox magic, would destroy Mincey's soul by claiming and despoiling the one pure thing in the degenerate's sad, sick and disgusting life.

The one thing Mincey Harris treasured the most.

The one thing he loved.

Darklord would claim Dandelion Dandelion.

And turn her into the biggest up-the-shitter slagbag in the world!

The evil black magician would use his terrible anal sorcery to seduce the girl who had brought some form of meaning and dignity into the heroin addict's sordid existence.

The magician threw back his head and laughed demonically in the tower room of his gothic eyrie high in the savage, black mountains of Bingley. The sinister magician started to crush some garlic and obscure herbs in a pestle and prepared his arse for the ceremony.

Pink Starfish hobbled into the sorcery room on crutches, his own gory bumhole hadn't healed properly from the savage attack by Strutter Sandanista but there was nothing wrong with his spunkhammer. Peter detested being on the receiving end of the sodomy but this was a piece of glamour work and the ancient rituals demanded that in instances of glamour magic the sorcerer himself had to be on the receiving end of the shitstabbing and Pink was hung like a field mouse so the ordeal wouldn't be too painful.

"Give yourself a good wanking first, Pink boy," ordered Darklord, defying the bass player to laugh at his ignoble position as he bent over a small pouffe in the middle of a crudely drawn pentagram.

"Just shove it in when you're nearly about to jizz, and don't fucking laugh! You're not the only bass player in the world you know!"

The bass player was finding the whole thing completely ridiculous but the money the retarded weirdo was paying stifled any derision in the wily gay bassist. Besides, a fuck's a fuck and Peter Darklord, despite being completely insane, was still rather dishy.

Pink nearly lost his boner, however, for as soon as he'd got his less than impressive danglepork up the nutter's chuffchute the mad arse magician started screaming and yelling in some weird language, pure exorcist shit, growling and doing some kind of horrific torn yodelling. It was a good job he'd hammered his pud up to the vinegar stroke thought Pink, or he doubted he'd be able to shoot off the babygrease.

As soon as Pink's watery jizz hit the shit, Darklord angrily crapped the bummer's bone out of his jacksie.

"Get out! Now!" screamed the singer, pulling up his velvet loon pants. "And remember! Not a word to anyone."

"Alright, Shirley, keep your wig on!" shot the bass player, regretting it instantly.

Fortunately for Pink and the ridiculous salary he was receiving, Darklord didn't seem to hear him.

He was utterly lost in a seething passion for vengeance!

Chapter Twenty Nine

Jesus Con Carne

Jesus Con Carne, Vice President of The Aztecs Of Sodom MC - the private guard of mega-handsome, super-intelligent, grand chessmaster and brilliant writer Zodiac Mindwarp - was getting mighty pissed off with his master's weirdo friend, the eccentric Bill Drummond, what the fuck was a brown magician anyway?

Jesus couldn't understand why they didn't just ride their hogs down to London to help Z's friend, the Leather Cowboy, Mincey Harris. But his duty wasn't to question but to obey. Obedience to something that had been earned and was worthy of his respect.

That thing was his admired commander Zodiac Mindwarp, retired rock God and all-round ultra fantastico.

The mighty Mexican biker, former president of the notorious Mexican outlaw bikers, Los Fuckeros, stroked the white scar on his left cheek and smiled. He remembered when Zodiac had whupped his ass in the Funky Shitlocker Cantina on the outskirts of Mexico city.

Jesus and eight Fuckeros were drinking beer when Zodiac wandered in. He was down in Mexico visiting his old bass player Tex Diablo, checking out some bullfighting action. Jesus couldn't recall how the fight started exactly but he remembered one of the Fuckeros, Burrito San Salvador, horsing around with one of the waitresses, well raping her actually when you think about it. That Zodiac cat man, he was like fucking lightning! He reached behind his neck and flung these small silver throwing knives, pinning Burrito and the rest of them

Fuckeros to the walls and floors. He flies in like Bruce fucking Lee, kicking and punching so fast you couldn't see the motherfucker. Wanking Jackie Fandango, the Fuckeros Sergeant at Arms, pulls out this monster hand cannon, a big silver Desert Eagle, getting the drop on Zed. Without blinking the wild rocker kicked the gun into the air, caught it on the way down, jammed it up against Jackie's face and blew the mother's head clean off, blood and bits of brain like baby teeth splattering all over the wall and bar. All the other Fuckeros were lying around bleeding and moaning, nursing broken arms and legs. The rocker turned towards Jesus and calmly combed his oily black hair, checking his reflection nonchalantly in the mirror behind the bar.

"Just you and me now, big guy..." said the singer.

Jesus saw the large black crucifix tattooed on the rocker's chest and, for the first time in his life, felt fear. There was something holy and terrible about the gringo. His eyes, as black as crude oil. shone in the dark cantina. They seemed to burn into the biker's very soul.

"Or are you gonna do the smart thing and walk away?"

Jesus knew that the singer knew that would be impossible. He was an outlaw biker, his honour would never allow it. But there was something else about Zodiac. Jesus liked him. How the fuck that was possible after he'd killed one of his companeros and beat the living shite out of the rest of them baffled him completely. It had to do with the respect that natural authority commands. Jesus knew the man was his better, something he'd never expected to meet in this life. He'd tolerated the commanders in the French Foreign legion, but here was a man he would gladly serve.

The duel was short.

Jesus bloodied the fierce rocker's nose which, judging by the amused and startled look on the man's face, had never happened before.

Zodiac punched the biker in the face, it felt like he'd been kicked in the teeth by a horse. The stunned biker was on his back.

"I could kill you now," said the strange mystic rocker, crouching over him and pointing the razor-sharp point of a beautiful Toledo dagger just below the biker's left eye. "Or you can choose to serve me".

The singer cut the Mexican below the eye and turned to walk out of the smashed Cantina, throwing a bunch of hundred dollar bills on the counter for the damage.

"Wait!" called the biker, mopping the blood from his face. Zodiac with his back to the man stopped in the doorway.

"I'll do whatever you say, hey, man, you're some far out cat, man, nobody ever beat me in a fight, man, nobody!"

The singer turned around smiling. That afternoon the fuckeros broke all the rules and had one hell of a three day leaving party for their President.

The recruitment of the rest of Zed's private guard took the next year and a half. The meanest, noblest and hardest men on the planet swore allegiance to the rocker king. Most of them Mexicans, from the hardest country on Earth, and all of them alive with the fiery spirit of Mexico's most famous son, the ultimate boxer, Roberto Duran.

When England fell into anarchy and bloody murder, which was coming any day now, all bikers know this, the rocker king would seize control of the kingdom, uniting the biker clans and implementing his dream to unite all of Europe and Russia to destroy those white devils who controlled the world - the American federal government with their ceaseless efforts at making the whole world as stupid as themselves.

But this Drummond cat, Jesus couldn't understand why his boss even talked to the fucking asshole, never mind seeming to respect him. The Scottish idiot was clearly insane. Jesus very nearly creamed the cunt when he found him doing his weird shitting magic up on the deck next to the biker's treasured Harley D. The gangly mong looked blankly through his cracked national health specs at the biker as he cussed him out for shitting next to the precious motorcycle. Z asked him politely to conduct his excromancy up on the front deck. The fucking barge thing stank as well, man. That shitting stuff wasn't like any sorcery he'd seen before. Mexican sorcerers used blood and skulls and stuff, but shit, man? It didn't connect. He respected his liege's judgement however and reluctantly passed on it, keeping up-wind of the flatulent Scot.

Bill Drummond couldn't understand why Z had insisted on bringing the big fucking beaner lunk along. It wasn't as if any violence was needed to reverse the stupid asshole Darklord's kindergarten Glamour spell. Arse magic was no contest for the Scotsman's ancient Excromantic shit magic. A few well placed turds on certain ley lines accompanied by a simple incantation and Mincey's love would be his once more. Why they needed the biker muscle was beyond him. If Zodiac knew something he wasn't saying.

The excromancer farted in a glass jar, sealed and labelled it.

Chapter Thirty

Clamjungle Pie

Mincey Harris couldn't remember being as happy in his entire life. Strutter was back in the band. Dandelion Dandelion, after a few minor hiccoughs, was back in his life. He loved her more than anything in the world. He was on a methadone programme, he was finally getting his shit together. There had been interest from Cosmosodomistic records. Frankie Auschwitz had finally seen sense and was determined to sign the band and completely ruin them.

The gig that night at Stinky Fingers rock club was rammed. Mincey and the boys performed their backstage ritual. Stood in a circle they mimed wanking off and jizzing all over the ceiling.

"Come on, man! Let's ROCK, man! Areeba reeba reba!" shouted Gerry Enchilada, his brickie's-crack peeping over the top of his bootcut jeans as they ran onto the small stage of the shitty Charing Cross toilet.

"Blow job Queen you know what I mean! She's outraaaaageous!" sang Strutter and Mince into the singer's mike. Mincey was doing his rooster walk and tongue-flickering thing with more enthusiasm than any of the band could remember. The audience roared their approval.

Mincey limbered up to the mike. already sweating heavily under the lights.

"This next one's dedicated to a kid we had the pleasure of knowing for a while but now he's rocking with Jimi and Jim, Kurt, Keith, Janice and all the rest in that big facking gig in the sky! Sonny Darklord, you were cool, man" said Mincey, soberly.

And then, screaming into the mike "But your old

man's a complete ARRRRRRSEHOLE!"

The band blasted into 'Fellatio Joe' from 'Booglerizer', their last but one album.

Peter Darklord seethed in the darkness at the back of the cramped hall. 'Fellatio Joe' had been one of his favourite Cowboys' songs. The rock star had to use all his energy to stop digging the inspired performance of his once favourite band. He slowly made his way through the sweaty throng to stand directly behind the abandoned figure of Dandelion Dandelion.

Dandy was dancing away like a madwoman, orgasming and singing along to the words.

"Fellatio Joe, Fellatio Joe, no one can blow like Fellatio Joe! Alright yeah baby, get down, wooh!"

So lost in the music was the young girl that she didn't notice the tall man behind her take a snippet of her hair and wank a great jizzoyster on to her shapely arse. Dandelion was so in love with the Mincer, she couldn't believe the mature singer felt the same way about her. For the past month it had felt like she was living in a fantasy, more like a film than the real world. Mincey, although she still thought he drank too much, had started on his methadone treatment and was attending the smokey rooms of Narcotics Anonymous to help him try to kick completely. He was being so brave!

When they weren't having the wildest sex imaginable - Mincey had even started fucking her in the cunt. They were painting the town all the colours of the rainbow, running through Regents Park laughing like children and drinking heavily, Dandelion laughingly trying to keep up with her beau, matching him drink for drink and then spewing her ring in the backs of cabs. Mincey was so funny when he blew chunks - that Tennents Super lager was strong stuff! And when he shat himself in Wardour Street, how they laughed and laughed! They both knew that Mincey probably needed help for his chronic alcoholism, but there was no rush, she was so proud of his succesful attempt at getting off the needle, all he had to do now was kick the methadone and keep going to meetings, her big brave man!

Dandelion couldn't believe it when Mincey wrote a song just for her - 'Clamjungle Pie'. It was so beautiful. Mincey had been drinking all day with Gerry, they were so funny sometimes, like little boys arguing over the last can of Tennants super. Of course Dandy sorted it all out and went and shoplifted a couple of sixpacks. When she got back she found that the the boys had had a little fight so she took their silly weapons off of them.

Gerry had broken a bottle over Mincey's head, blood from a head wound dripped from the end of his nose.

"You focking beetch, man, I keel you!" said the overweight Mexican lunging at Mincey with his silver switchblade.

Of course the beaner missed, fell over and somehow managed to stab himself up his own arse. When the wrecked duo spotted the Tennents their argument was forgotten and they happily ripped off the ring pulls and caned themselves into oblivion, what a pair! A couple of hours later they were both asleep. The beaner had shat himself and Mincey had been sick all over the carpet. She dragged the unconscious singer into their bed where she flipped a piece of regurgitated carrot off his bottom lip and kissed him on the mouth.

She awoke early the next morning to find Mince sat on the end of the bed, his hair and chest still covered in dried spew, bits of donor kebab meat and regurgitated cabbage stuck to his skinny body. She listened as he strummed his acoustic guitar, singing quietly to himself

"She's my Clamjungle pie, Clamjungle, Clamjungle pie, oh yes" he hummed away. And then he sang the words that made her cry.

"Dandy, oh Dandelion you're my Clamjungle pie, clamjungle jungle, babe, I want to bungle in your jungle, Clamjungle, no one smokes my horn as good as little Clamjungle, Clamjungle pie..."

The singer put down his guitar and went to the toilet,

she laughed as her man took a noisy, farting, squittering dump, humming the tune to himself as he dropped his boulders and soup.

"Fucking and sucking, Sucking and a fucking, my little clamjungle, Clamjungle pie, alright, wooh," he sang quietly to himself as he got back into bed with Dandy. Dandy pretended to be asleep as her romantic lover started fucking her tenderly up the arsehole.

Tonight was going to be the first time the band were to play her song live. She was electric with excitement, orgasming all over the place, her knickers were soaking wet and she wondered if anybody had noticed. Not that she cared anyway.

Suddenly she recognised the opening chords of her song, Mincey looked her straight in the eye.

"This one's for a very special lady," he said over the intro.

Dandelion wanted to shit she was so happy.

By the time the band had reached the chorus she'd experienced an orgasm for every line.

"Clamjungle, Clamjungle, let me bungle, baby, in your clamjungle! wooh alright, Strutter baby!"

Mincey smiled at his wild guitarist, Strutter, who was enjoying himself so much he'd got his cock out.

"Come on baby, bungle my jungle baby! Alright!"

Strutter peeled into a mad solo, wangbarring up and down like a flaming Stuka divebombing innocent civilians, chopping out ultrafast rhythms and wild harmonics. It was Strutter's finest hour, his face contorting beneath the fiery lights, his cock flying all over the place as he ran around the stage like a flaming turkey. It was going to be a tough number to follow, so they dragged out an old favourite, the Cowboy classic 'Lesbian Tamer' - Gerry Enchilada's paean to stuck up bitches who played hard to get.

"Lesbian Tamer, Lesbian Tamer, bend over, baby, I'm gonna tame ya! Gonna Tame ya, I'm a Lesbian tamer! Alright suck it suck it suck it!"

Mincey bawled out the lines as he ran around the stage, flashing his skinny arse and getting his cock out, waggling it in the girls' faces down the front. Gerry was playing one handed, the music had sent him wild, he not only had his cock out, he was mashing it big time, his face screwed up with mad lust. As the band crashed through their final songs, the tugging Mexican spurted out a massive glob of sourcream all over a couple of 14-year-old teenyboppers down at the front of the stage.

This was the best performance Dandy had ever seen. She wanted to run backstage immediately and fellate Mincey's very soul out through his bell-end but there was no way the crowd were going to let them go without at least one encore. Gerry walked out on stage, his big Mexican cock still hanging out, a clear viscous string of jizz slime hanging off the end.

"Hey Amigos!" he shouted down the mike "You want more of thees sheet, man? You gonna have to focking shout louder man, I cannot heeeeer you, man!"

The crowd went berserk, chicks had started throwing their knickers onto the stage, Gerry caught a pair and held them to his face, sniffing deeply on the soaking gusset.

"Hey, mama, what you doing here, man? I recognise the smell of my mother's big fat beaner gash anywhere, man!" he joked and then started hammering the bass solo intro as the rest of the cowboys took up their instruments and powered into Bumfucker.

They were fantastic.

Mincey got his cock out.

Dandelion gasped.

It was erect, his big fat pork sword for all the world to see. She felt intensely jealous as he let some teenybopper bitches down the front suck him off during 'Blow Job Queen' but she tamed the destructive feelings, it was just a part of the performance, she reasoned. The band powered to a climax, Robbie spunking all over his bass drum and kicking his kit over, masturbating insanely, eyes way back in their sockets. The beaner and Strutter were also wanking furiously, covering the chicks down at the front in a great shower of monkey-juice.

Mincey was up on the PA rig getting sucked off by a 14 year old teenybopper. He pulled his dick out at the crucial moment and shot his great geyser of jizz all over the audience. Mincey was the most copious jizzer she'd ever seen, the stud pumped out at least two pints of spamjuice, drenching the screaming chicks down at the front.

Dandelion was racing down the labyrinth of passages backstage when she saw him.

The mysterious Peter Darklord.

She felt dizzy, something strange was happening to her.

The tall man was wearing a top hat and a long black cape.

He slowly pulled back the black velvet cloak and turned around to reveal his smooth alabaster arse to the confused Dandelion. Before she knew what she was doing she was on her knees, kissing the Black Magician's backside, wiggling her tongue up into the cool satanic butthole.

Darklord turned around and she fell on his sinister blood hammer, sucking on his deep purple as if her life depended on it.

"That's enough, Dandelion, for now. Off your knees, girl, quickly, follow me. I have a car waiting."

Dandy felt as if her entire world had imploded. This terrifying need from out of the blue to be with Peter Darklord had completely and instantaneously eclipsed her feelings for Mincey Harris. The dark master swept her along the corridor, past a shocked looking Gerry Enchilada who was porking a drugged up teenybopper.

"Hey man, what you doing with Mincey's chick, man?" said the burly Mexican, his cock hanging out of his dirty yellow minibriefs as he tried to grab hold of the arrogant Darklord.

"Out of my way you fool!" sneered the Tramps of Dawn front man, pushing the Mexican backwards, making him fall over, the tangled jeans around his ankles.

"Hey, man, you focking fock! Fock you, man! You

asshole, man!! I'm gonna tell Mincey, man!"

Dandelion stopped dead in her tracks and turned back to the humiliated Mexican who was desperately trying to pull his pants up.

"Gerry," she said, her voice unusually cold, there was something different about her, even the dimwitted Enchilada could see that, "tell Mincey not to try and find me. It's over. I love Peter now."

Without a pause, Dandy turned on her heel and joined the smirking Darklord.

"Hey, man!" he shouted. "You put a focking spell on her, man! Or focking something, man, you focking asshole! I'm gonna tell Mincey, man!"

The couple ignored him and stepped out into the night and into Darklord's gothic looking black stretch-limo. They sped into the night, up the deserted M1 towards Darklord's castle high in the black Bingley mountains.

"After you finish off my boney-maroney, chicquita baby, heh heh, oh yeah, suck uncle Gerry's purple hot chilli pepper baby, yeah ooh yeah baby mmmmm tha's good, man...." The Mexican forgot about Darklord and blorped all over the young girl's tonsils, the poor thing immediately puked.

"Hey you fockin' little beetch, them's my bes' leather trousers, man, oh fock..." He grabbed hold of the girl's hair and started wiping the vomit off his pants with it, the poor thing started crying into Gerry's sweaty balls...

Chapter Thirty One

The Faggots of Destruction

Mincey was devastated. He couldn't believe it, how long had that fucking cunt been fucking Darklord? Why had she led him along all this time? But there was something wrong. Usually, when a slut's been fucking around, all the suspicions fall into place, your paranoia finally justified. Telephones being hung up when the bitch doesn't answer, new hairstyles, pathetic excuses and overnight stays at sisters, mothers and all kinds of friends you've never heard of, all kinds of petty little bitch pointers that you ignored, usually because you couldn't give a fuck. But no, Dandy had been with him the whole time since the embarrassing Arse Johnson incident, there was something seriously wrong.

He was back on the smack of course, a major relapse, but even that cure all and comforter of everything couldn't help, even beneath the sedation of the red flowers, she was still there, like a vast scorching desert.

Dandelion Dandelion, he began the letter before screwing it up and throwing it amongst the mountain of other screwed up bits of paper.

It was his old friend, the king of rock music and fantastic sex, Zodiac Mindwarp, whose face he saw when he resurfaced from his suicide attempt. Mincey had tried to hang himself from the top of the stairs.

A huge Mexican biker was pushing on his chest to restart his heart and a creepy looking guy in broken NHS gegs smelling of farts lurked in the background, pissing around with star charts and what looked like a bucket of shit.

"Oh fack, Zode man, what the fack are....what's that facking smell?" coughed the embarrassed Mincer.

"Looks like we got here just in time" said Z calmly. "That Darklord asshole, he's put Dandy under some cockeyed, arse magic glamour spell!" continued his noble friend authoritatively, making Mincey feel reassured and ashamed at the same time. Reassured because now he knew that Dandy hadn't betrayed him, ashamed because he'd doubted her love for him in the first place. A cockeyed, arse magic, glamour spell! Why hadn't he thought of that!

"Oh my God!" shouted the stinky guy Mincey didn't recognise. "Oh by the daemons of Excromancy! He's performed a rising!" Bill held a turd in his hands, brandishing it in Z and Jesus Con Carne's direction.

"The Faggots Of Destruction!"

Z and Jesus looked confused.

"This is much more serious than I thought!" added the turd magician seriously.

"What the fuck's he talking about. man?" said the humongo biker. "And get that fucking turd out of my face, man! Fuck! It stinks man!"

Bill placed the sloppy turd on Mincey's table.

"Look, here. The cracks here, and the peanuts. One second..." Bill cut the turd in two and studied the inside of his occult piece of shit, prodding it with a pencil "This clump of pale brown and this black arse stone..."

"I'm afraid it doesn't mean anything to me, old friend" said Z. "A turd's a turd to me, but I respect your erudition and arcane wisdom in these affairs. So what exactly are the Faggots Of Destruction?"

"Homosexual elementals, it's arse magic stuff. Darklord is a much more efficient Black Arse magician than I thought, this stuff is way up on the 23 Adept Belial, 23 degrees east of the Constructs of the original Bummers Of The Universe level," said Bill, seeming to know what he was talking about.

"You can tell all that just by looking at a lump of shit,

man?" said Jesus, a tone of wary respect creeping into his voice.

"Unfortunately yes, it's not much, were going to have to reverse the glamour spell first and then deal with the Faggots Of Destruction when we come across them," said Bill, concentrating hard.

"What the fack's he on about, man, and why's he facking shitting on my coffee table?" said Mincey. Apart from the rope burn round his neck, he seemed pretty much recovered.

"Mr Harris," Bill addressed the singer authoratively, "we'll need a stool sample"

"A what?"

"A piece of your shit," answered the Excromancer, tetchily

"What the fack for? You facking pervert!" spat Mincey, suspecting that the brown magician was trying to drag him into some weird spamfancying buggery game.

"Do you want Dandelion back? Or are you content to let Darklord keep her?"

"Of course I want..." started Mincey before being cut short by the vexed magician.

"Then give me a turd now, here, in this jar, quickly for God's sake! It's a simple reversal but we must act promptly, the longer she remains under the glamour, the harder it is to reverse the spell!"

Mincey looked at Z who nodded calmly. The rocker unfastened his pants and nipped off a hard black one. The heroin had made him terribly constipated so it took a while, poor Mincey, straining like a three-year-old on his potty.

Bill was flipping through his magickal A-to-Z of London, it was like an ordinary A-to-Z except, along with all the roads and train lines, it contained an extremely intricate crossweaving of all the ley lines that ran through or began in London. Hundreds of them.

"Aha, we're in luck!" said the pungent turd genius. "The three ley lines we need, the ones that run beneath Darklord's castle in the Bingley mountains, are all within a few miles from here."

Bill examined the black turd in the specimen jar and nodded. "I'll be back within the hour".

The shit magician hesitated at the door. "If any of the Faggots Of Destruction turn up, ignore them completely, don't get into any dialogue with them, that's exactly what they want. They're fairly harmless, they may have slight poltergeist powers but it's your head they want to fuck with. Whistle or sing a song, just don't talk to them. Z knows how to perform a banishment, don't you Z?"

"It's been a while, my occult powers may be a little rusty, but yes, a banishment is fairly simple, I'm sure we'll be OK,'" said the calm and majestically composed god of a man.

Chapter Thirty Two

Domestos Enema

Tara Emerson Lake Dogshit-Ffuck-ffeatures, the aristocratic girlfriend of Peter Darklord, was experiencing sensations she had always felt were beneath her. Envy. How could an aristocrat, with the blood of Kings and Queens flowing through her veins, possibly feel envy? Wasn't an aristocrat a perfect example of her race? Her entire education had reiterated this fact, told her over and over again that she was an elevated person. That she shone like a star, high above the common herd. For all of her 26 years she had firmly believed this to be axiomatic.

So artificial and received was her image of herself and so firmly lodged within her sensibilities, the young Tara had somehow felt emboldened to step outside the castle walls of her pampered existence with only her nobility to guard her.

Peter Darklord had arrived at a similar self-image, albeit through a more direct form of delusion, the man was simply insane.

Tara's self-confidence however had been shattered recently by the presence within the gloomy shadows of Peter Darklord's gothic home Gormenghast, high in the Bingley mountains, by a rare flower of a girl, a trembling beauty of a thing, Dandelion Dandelion.

Here truly was a genuine aristos of the human species, one that was completely natural. Her innate superiority was much more real than the shoddy combination of inbreeding, money and insecure snobbery that passes for today's aristocracy.

Tara hated her.

Since Dandelion's arrival at Gormenghast, Tara (the spoiled flatchested daddy's girl) had stayed in her room, masturbating anxiously and taking huge amounts of cocaine, swilled down with champagne.

Her boyfriend, Peter Darklord, hadn't even bothered to explain what the hateful girl was doing up here in the black mountains of West Yorkshire. But she'd recognized the look in the girl's eyes when she spied on them in Peter's bedroom.

It was love. But not a natural love. Her decadent boyfriend had obviously entrapped the little bitch inside one of his glamour spells. That was how it had started with herself and her lord and master, Peter Darklord, all those sperm-drenched years ago when she was no older than the little tart being currently impaled on Peter's guthammer.

Tara was a furnace of white hot loathing and scalding hatred for the younger woman. Woman? She was still a girl, despite the clashing magnificence of her firm teenage breasts.

Tara bided her time. Around midnight Peter would start to work, composing one of his epic progressive rock symphonies, writing poetry or studying his grimoires.

The girl had been there just under a week when Tara's emotional chemistry was finally stoked beyond boiling point by the cocaine and alcohol. After she'd seen Peter head off to his recording bunker in the northern acres of Gormenghast's bare blasted grounds, the demented drunken devil-bitch aristocrat set off for the tower in the western wing of the huge rambling pile.

She kicked open the door of Dandelion's room and screamed at the girl, grabbing her by her long black hair and slamming her up against a wall. Dandy was taken completely by surprise, who the fuck was this insane bitch? Why was she pissed off with her? A bright white light was the last thing she saw - the second after the mad woman had brought down the solid gold phallus across her cheek.

Dandelion thought she had wet the bed when she surfaced from her concussion. She shook her head and tried to move her limbs. She couldn't. She saw the mad woman who'd attacked her earlier, what the fuck was happening? Where was... she almost said Mincey to herself but suddenly remembered that it was Peter she loved now. Where was Peter? And who was this fucking lunatic smiling down at her?

"Are we awake my pretty pretty?" asked the madwoman. She was sitting on a wooden stool threading a needle and cotton. Dandelion was naked, spread eagled on a wooden St Andrews cross, her cunt felt dangerously exposed.

Dandy almost fainted when the mad woman started to sew up her bucket. Her screams bounced off the stone walls and ceiling. It was as if the crazy bitch was using a blow torch on her. Tara Emerson Lake Dogshit Ffuck-ffeatures laughed cruelly as the little bitch screamed beneath her needle.

"I'll teach you to steal my man, you whore!"

She spat in Dandy's face.

As the last stitch closed up Dandy's gash, down in London Bill Drummond placed a piece of Mincey's black turd on the final leyline at the junction of Great Eastern Street and Old Street. In terms of interstellar and terrestrial ley-lines this place is like a cosmic Clapham junction, lines from all over the galaxy intercross at this powerful spot. The brown magician pulled up his kilt and shat on top of Mincey's small black turd. He danced around the ordure, performing his Farts Of The Four Winds, called on the Gods Of Excrement and stamped down hard on the pile of shit, splattering the mess all over the front of the Foundry pub.

As the shit hit the window, up in the Bingley mountains, Dandy called out for Mincey, her mind a whirlpool of confusion and shadows. The arse magic glamour spell had been lifted. Her cruel tormentress, Dogshit Ffuck-ffeatures, threw back her head, her harsh laughter richocheting into the high vaulted ceiling of her prison.

"So, you little slut! Someone has lifted the glamour! We are a popular little bitch, aren't we!" she said, pure malevolent evil burning in her black eyes. Dandy had no idea what this mad Cruella De Ville was rambling about. The pain burning her cunt was excruciating, it felt as if she was being fucked by The Human Torch. Flame fucking off! Please God! She was becoming delirious, her confused mind spinning like an evil carousel with demons instead of horses. Her tormentress had cut her from the cross and strapped her down across what appeared to be a butchers slab.

Poor Dandelion passed out completely when the bitch started in with the Domestos enema.

Where was Mincey? Why hadnt he tried to save her? She screamed in agony as her torturer started stuffing stinging nettles up her burning arsehole. The arsehole that Mincey loved so much.

"OH MINCEY!" she screamed as Tara Emerson Lake Dogshit Ffuck-ffeatures laughed cruelly at her agony.

Chapter Thirty Three

The Black Mountains Of Bingley

"If we sail at full steam and there are no engine problems we should make it in just under three weeks" said brown magician Bill, referring to his narrow barge The Hysterical Bitch.

"Are you out of your facking mind!?" shouted the distraught Mincey. "We can be there in two facking hours if we burn up the M1!"

"One hour," said Jesus, "on bikes."

"Have you ever come across an elemental before?" replied Bill, pushing his cracked glasses up his nose.

"What the fack is he talking about, man?" shouted the increasingly anxious Mincey.

"I think my excromantic friend is referring to The Faggots Of Destruction, am I right, old boy?" questioned the sage ex rocker Zodiac.

"Exactly. Darklord has risen four Faggots Of Destruction. Individually they are easily banishable but if they decide to attack all together, which I'm sure they will, then we will need all the equipment I have stored on my narrow barge." The Scottish magician obviously knew what he was talking about.

The odd bunch boarded The Hysterical Bitch which was berthed in London's Little Amsterdam at Camden town and hauled anchor. A crowd of weirdo goths with Frankenstein piercings and black clothes recognised Zodiac and ran along the bank shouting after the handsome sexual genius, they were trying to give him money and wanted to have sex with him. Jesus killed all seven of them with his Mexican martial arts skills, which is basically just knife violence. When it came to his master's safety Jesus acted first and thought later. The black haired girls bled to death outside Dingwalls, they seemed to enjoy it, all the blood and stuff made them look like a vampire film. Very gothic.

Three weeks passed with no sight or sound of The Faggots Of Destruction. The tension on the small narrow boat was reaching breaking point, Mincey was going out of his mind and was dangerously low on skag.

"I've arranged for the men to meet us at The Fuhrer's Head, a small bar in Ilkley town centre" said Zodiac.

"I'm sure Darklord will have plenty of security guards, but the Aztecs will be more than sufficient to deal with any problems we have getting into Darklord's castle; Gormenghast," he added, referring to his private biker army, The Aztecs of Sodom.

"It's been a while since they've spilled serious blood, no doubt they'll be impatient for some scarlet action," he continued.

He was right as well, it had been nearly two months since the Aztecs had returned from Africa. Although they had sworn allegiance and loyalty till death to Mindwarp, their overlord would hire out his army on a regular basis to clean up the many wars in the underdeveloped countries. It kept them sharp, and maintained their violence skills in tip top form, far better than any training could. In over 40 anti-government coups and civil wars all over Africa, The Aztecs of Sodom had lost not one single man. They made the SAS look like the bunch of public school fairies that they were.

They were two days away from the dread mountains of Bingley, that towering jagged range, when The Faggots Of Destruction showed up.

The battle was short but fierce, the shit literally flying in all directions.

Bill had painted talismans in his own ordure all over the barge for protection. The elementals were truly horrible, humanoid in shape, dressed in homosexual costumes - skinhead, sailor, leatherman, construction worker. They hovered in the air circling the barge, masturbating their ridiculously large penises and calling out cattish insults to Bill and his crew.

"What the fucking hell are they?" said Jesus. The fearless Aztec appeared disturbed, a rare thing for this giant of a man. The floating monsters would join together in a writhing ball of buggering, fellating anal confusion then drift apart again, ugly cocks spurting devil jizz all over the barge's portholes.

"Originally, you won't believe this, but they were angels," said Bill keeping a wary eye on the floating black magic bummers, circling around The Hysterical Bitch.

"But they backed the wrong team when the war in heaven raged, they fell with their commander, that damned arch angel that once sat at God's right hand, Lucifer, the light bringer."

" You mean they're Demons?" asked the monster biker.

"No, they're fallen angels. Demons are a cinch to banish. These fuckers? We'll just have to pray to the Gods Of Excrement that my magic works," said Bill stripping himself naked and covering himself from head to toe in shit. The intense magician started to masturbate furiously, chanting in Latin, gathering his magickal tools together.

"All of you get in the back, I'm going up on deck, if I fall..." the Scotsman smiled as he opened the hatch. "I'll see you in Hell!"

The brave brown-magician battled hard with the homosexual elementals, throwing turds at them, screeching his banishment incantations, cursing them in long forgotten languages and farting loudly in their general direction. He kept up a furious rate of turkey punishment, battering all hell out of his penis and eventually spraying the fallen angels with ridiculously copious amounts of jizz. One by one they fell, the shit magic causing them to burst into flames as they returned to Hell covered in shit and screaming like banshees.

An exhausted Drummond stumbled into the galley, opening a bottle of cheap scotch with trembling hands and chugging deeply on the fiery liquid.

"Hey, man," said the huge biker, Jesus Con Carne. "I'll never rag you about your shit magic again, man. You can shit in my house, shit on my hog, anything man, you were fucking awesome!" he said, genuinely impressed and shaking Bill's shitty hand.

The brown magician was exhausted, elemental banishment, as any magician worth his wand knows, drains the lifeforce at an alarming rate. The Scottish magician had selflessly sacrificed several years from the end of his life during the banishment. At one stage during the ritual it had felt as if the macho Scottish sorcerer was about to be drawn down the spinning black vortex he'd shat into existence, straight into Hell itself. But, squeezing out his last stool and brandishing it at the Leatherman, and farting as if his life depended on it, he managed to hang on by the skin of his bell end.

The Faggots Of Destruction were gone, back to Hell - until some other idiot rose them.

Chapter Thirty Four

20 Inch Spamjagger

The Aztecs of Sodom MC freewheeled down from the bleak Pennines like some battle-ready horde from the Dark Ages. Festooned with jangling swastikas and Iron crosses, wearing impenetrable mirror shades and sinister nazi helmets covered in weird psychedelic design, they glided into the small town of Ilkley like death's black angels.

Despite the freezing winds high on the barren Yorkshire tundra these magnificent bikers wore only black leather waistcoats over their hirsute tattooed torsos. Hundreds of macabre designs were carved into their proud flesh; SS runes, devils, naked women, snakes and the French Foreign Legion devil's guard badge - a muscular forearm appearing from a cloud clutching a winged dagger with the legend MARCH OR DIE inscribed above and below it.

Their back patch colours reflected the Mexican heritage of these French Foreign legion veterans. Beneath the top rocker which spelt out AZTECS in fiery letters a heart dripping blood was surrounded by a blazing Mithran sun, a reference to their Aztec ancestor's bloody sacrifices. That proud ancient warrior race believed that unless the sun was fed a steady stream of still beating hearts, ripped from living victims, it would refuse to rise the following morning. The bottom rocker spelt out the terrifying words OF SODOM - a reference to military homosexuality, male rape being a traditional feature of extreme warfare as practiced since the days of the Spartans. The SAS, America's Navy Seals and the Israeli Mossad are just a few of the crack units that practice this dreadful anal martial art.

It was early evening when the Aztecs entered The Fuhrer's Head pub.

Melvyn Frankenstein, the landlord of The Fuhrer's Head felt an icicle of terror spear him in the guts as the fearsome bike warriors entered the front door of his popular pub and ordered beer, his hands were shaking as he pulled forty pints of Old Dogshit bitter, a strong local brew. The men were admiring the unique collection of Third Reich paraphenalia that decorated the walls. There were swastika flags, SS standards, collections of medals and daggers and, in pride of place above the fireplace. a huge oil painting of Adolf Hitler himself, the Fuhrer's cold black eyes staring into some imagined destiny that only he could understand.

The Nazi theme was his father's idea, there were more Irish bars scattered around the world than there were in Ireland itself and Melvyn wanted something more original. The brewery were a little concerned at first but backed off when it proved to be very popular with the conservative locals as well as the elderly German tourists who visited Yorkshire regularly to see the places and meet the people they had bombed during the war.

Melvyn's father, Oswald Frankenstein, had been a guard at the notorious Belsen concentration camp and had resettled in Bradford after the war, fleeing the communists. After all the fuss had died down, Oswald had arranged to have all of his uniforms and flags, daggers etc flown over to England.

The bikers seemed to be impressed by the collection, studying a huge oil painting of The Fuhrer dressed in teutonic armour astride a white horse. Melvyn relaxed a little when he noticed the reichian decorations attached to the fierce bikers leather waistcoats.

"You too are admirers of the Fuhrer?" he asked Rapeman Rape nervously as he passed the massive tattooed biker his beer. The giant looked down at Melvyn, surprised at the man's forwardness. People didn't usually talk to The Aztecs, their ferocious appearance usually commanded a silent respect.

"We don't admire anyone or anything except our own Fuhrer, Zodiac, " answered the biker in a deep submarine voice that dripped malice and cool intimidation. "And violence," he finished, taking off his mirror shades and fixing the uppity little Nazi shit with a steely blue death stare.

Melvyn Frankenstein said nothing.

He could feel his legs shaking beneath him.

He had just shit his pants.

He could feel the hot log steaming and hanging low in his underpants.

No one offered to pay for the forty pints and Melvyn wasn't going to ask for it.

He rushed up to the bathroom to wash his arse and change his pants.

It was midnight when Zodiac, Mincey, Bill and Jesus entered The Fuhrer's Head. The bikers welcomed their leader and vice president with a drunken and raucous bonhomie. The bike warriors had been drinking hard for six hours and were pretty much rat arsed. They'd finished off all the beer and were making their way through the many optics lined along the wall behind the bar. Zodiac noticed the dead bodies immediately and smiled indulgently. Nailed to the wall, nine cops, all with their pants removed, blood and shit leaking from their ripped sphincters.

"What's with the Christmas decorations?" said Jesus unconcernedly, nodding towards her majesty's finest, the Aztecs killed cops like other people killed flies.

"The stupid assholes tried to bust up our party, man." answered Stonebollocks Chillipepper, a mean looking Aztec with a lunar landscape of a face, ravaged by industrial strength acne when he was a teenager. "That little focker on the bar man, cocksucker made a big mistake man, calling the cops man, focking stupid thing to die for, a few beers man." He pointed at the dead body of Melvyn Frankenstein, laying across the bar. The poor bastard's arse was ripped half way up his back, it was obviously the work of Horsecock Satan, the mega-dicked Aztec with the 20 inch spamjagger.

"Nice bar!" said Jesus ironically, admiring a

particularly gruesome picture of some death camp ovens, it showed Melvyn's father, Oswald Frankenstein in his SS guard's uniform smiling at the camera, the feet of two dead bodies extending from the gory mouths of those hellish ovens. "To Melvyn, love Dad" was inscribed in the corner.

"That's Melvyn, I take it?" said Zodiac, pointing at the arse ravaged barman.

"Yeah man, I did him good man, look at his focking asshole man!" laughed Horsecock Satan, as he polished up his penis with surgical spirits and vinegar. Horsecock Satan looked after his ferocious bitch hammer like a boxer looks after his fists.

"Ilkley's a weird fucking place," mused Zodiac, probing Melvyn's arse with his ebony swagger stick and picking up an empty canister of Zyklon B that was being used as an ash tray.

"Fucking weird, it doesn't surprise me people round here would dig a place like this..." said the super-intellectual rocker, replacing the gory souvenir on the bar. "You wouldn't believe the number of escaped Nazi collaborators from the former captive nations, Lithuania, Latvia etc who ended up in West Yorkshire. From here to Bradford, fucking thousands of them..." he added absentmindedly to no one in particular.

Chapter Thirty Five

The Dead Murderers Society

Dandelion Dandelion just wished her captors would kill her and have done with it.

For three weeks she'd been tortured and beaten every day. Darklord and the horrible Ffuck-ffeatures woman seemed to be using her torture as some depraved form of foreplay.

What kind of evil perverts would do this to another human being? She felt the hot tears sting as they ran from her two black eyes down her hideously swollen and lacerated face. The bastards had pulled out all of her teeth, she could see them scattered around on the floor like pieces of broken china, the dried blood was still caked around her mouth and across her ruined breasts. Yesterday Tara Ffuck-ffeatures, the flat-chested uberbitch, had sliced off Dandy's nipples and wittily stitched them onto her buttocks, making some remark about tits and arses in the same bra. Darklord laughed out loud at his sick girlfriend's little torture joke.

There was something terribly, insanely wrong with the man. He thought it great sport to attach four or five leather rings studded with sharp metal spikes and hooks around his dick and then ram his ugly cock hard into the innocent girl's arse until the pain rendered her unconscious. Mincey loved Dandy's arsehole, with the Domestos enema and the daily spike buggering it was now probably beyond repair, just a ragged and torn hole that couldn't hang on to its shit. Runny faeces and black blood trickled down the back of her legs collecting in a stinking puddle at her feet, the smell was eyeball scraping - bleach, blood, diarrhoea, vomit and piss. It smelled like a Calcutta curry house khazi.

Her sobs wracked her tortured body, she was hanging

from her wrists attached to the wooden St Andrews cross, alone in the darkness when suddenly light flooded into the room. It was the perverted duo in for their daily sexual torture session, laughing and quaffing breakfast champagne.

"I don't think the bitch is going to last much longer, Peter darling.." said Tara Emerson Lake Dogshit Ffuck-ffeatures as she fished around in Darklord's leather trousers for his evil penis.

"Nonsense, dear girl, we've only just started! My my!" he said, removing his leather trousers and casually masturbating as he wandered behind Dandelion's black and blue body.

"Those nipples have taken excellently, how ridiculous she looks, such an inspired idea Tara my love, what wit you possess!" chuckled the sadist.

"I hope you've brought your sewing kit again darling, I had a super idea this morning during my ablutions" he continued, sticking something cold up Dandy's ragged and bleeding backside.

"Of course, Peter my sweet, I never leave home without it. Mummy always stressed upon me to always be prepared, you never know when you might come across an innocent torture victim!"

The sight of Dandelion's ruined body had excited Tara so much she had her hands down the front of her rubber knickers and was mashing away on her clitoris. She fired off a small climax and produced a small silver sewing kit from her cunt.

"What hellish needlework are we going to be doing today, beloved master?" she asked, dropping to her knees.

Darklord casually pissed in her mouth and she orgasmed again.

"I thought we could stitch this onto our little friend." The uberbuggerist removed a severed penis from his rubber smoking jacket pocket and threw it onto the floor.

"Oh darling how witty, you are such a genius!" trilled the flat-chested aristocrat

"And where were you thinking of placing it? What about slicing off her nose and sewing it there, we could call her fuck face!" Tara laughed loudly at her own joke.

"So Jake and Dinos Chapman!" she laughed again at her little art joke, Peter was very keen on the two London weirdos artwork and had dozens of the pair's grotesque sculptures all over the house. Tara picked up the severed penis, it was overly large and looked familiar.

"Where did you get it from? It's still warm, the blood still fresh," asked Tara, sucking the blood out through the jap's-eye, savouring the coppery taste and washing it down with yet more champagne.

"A donation from one of the security guards, I didn't like the way he was looking at me, what's his name? The one in the kitchen, Rawbone Fartgristle or something?"

"Oh, of course, I thought I recognized it, he's buggered me a number of times and I never forget a penis, I must say, it looked better on him..", she answered, pulling the skin back and licking again on the salty blood leaking from the urethra.

"Give it to me my love, you'll like this..". Peter giggled creepily and took the severed pork from his perverted lover, he placed it over Dandy's sewn-up gash.

"What do you think? Our own little sex-change boy!"

Tara went into a fit of giggles as she pinned the cock on to Dandy's suppurating cunt, it was badly infected with septacaemia and had started leaking yellow and green pus.

"You're a genius, Darklord!" said the wealthy perve. "A bloody genius, Ian Brady had nothing on you!" She cackled again and started sewing the severed danglepork onto the girls sick pudenda.

As a young girl, Tara had a serious crush on Ian Brady, the repulsive Moors Murderer famous for murdering, raping and torturing very small children. Along with his ghoulish lover, Myra Hindley, they'd made tapes of the little ones' suffering and pleas for mercy, calling for their mothers while being sexually abused by the fiendish couple.

It was fashionable at Sherbourne - the elite and expensive girls school she attended - to write to murderers imprisoned for life for their appaling crimes. A certain kudos was afforded the girls who received letters from the most depraved of all these vile specimens of inhumanity.

The young schoolgirls would send nude photographs of themselves and soiled knickers to tempt this human dross into writing back. Almost all of the masturbating monsters replied by first post, often sending plastic bags of their sperm and pubic hair, along with the invariable request for the young girls to swallow the sperm and sniff the pubic hair. Extra points, of course, were awarded to those girls who received murderer sperm in the mail.

Tara had had dozens of warped penpals including the Yorkshire Ripper, who had mailed her well over over a pint of his evil semen. She'd washed it down with oysters and champagne, it hadn't tasted particularly evil, just a little tart, and salty. She'd put that down to the prison diet her poor penfriend had to contend with.

But it was handsome Ian whose letters she loved the most. It was Ian who first got her interested in murder and torture.All day she would read and reread the sophisticated aesthete's beautiful letters, he was so, so intelligent and wise. He made her head spin with his long, handwritten letters about love and Hitler and Nietzchze. She would drink his sperm samples greedily after she finished her billets doux and daydream about murdering small children with him, taking picnics above the bodies of their victims buried on Saddleworth moor, making passionate love, buggering and fellating as they listened to some sexy tape recordings of their own. Oh Ian, she would sigh, staring at his photograph - you're just misunderstood my baby, the world wasn't ready for a man so forceful and free, so dynamic and so alive as you.

Wouldn't it be wonderful, she thought, tucked up in her Sherbourne bed, if one day he was released! She'd meet him at the prison gates with his favourite black shirt and a tape recorder. The two of them in matching black shirts and sunglasses would frolic across those beautiful barren moors murdering and torturing small children to their hearts' content. Ah, if only......

At school, while all the other girls were doing boringly normal things like dating pop stars and having anal sex with each other's fathers, Tara formed her own little society. She got the idea from the film The Dead Poets Society, only hers was much better, The Dead Murderers Society - it had a certain ring to it she thought.

The Dead Murderers Society would meet in the woods on the edge of the school grounds. The five friends would read accounts of the most evil murderers that ever stalked the planet, drink absinthe and jack up hard drugs. Of course Jack the Ripper was a perennial favourite, the five girls would delight in the story of saucy Jacky and the final murder of Mary Kelly. Pictures of the hideously mutilated Mary would be passed around and examined beneath their maglites, sliced up like a pig she was, breasts removed and placed on the bedside table. Thighs, eyes, buttocks, intestines, unravelled and festooned around the walls like Christmas in hell. The young girls would giggle in delight at the delicious horror of it all. Somehow, probably because they all came from such wealthy upper class families, the girls thought it perfectly alright to slaughter the poor. What on Earth were the masses there for if not to provide sport for their betters? And biologically of course, a prostitute is't really that different from a stag or a fox...certainly not as beautiful, that was for sure.

Ed Gein, the midwest cannibal who inspired the movies Psycho and The Texas Chainsaw Massacre was another favourite. Where Jemima Arserippeer-Assetstripper got all the police photographs from, goodness only knows. Gein's house looked like something from the most evil pits of hell. All his furniture was made from human body parts. He'd tailored a ghastly little waistcoat from one of his dead neighbours, it had breasts, the girls giggled uncontrollably at the deranged killer's style. Amazing!

As was the story of Albert Fish. the ultimate American meta-pervert. The little old man who looked like a kindly old grandfather but was in reality probably one of the sickest men that ever lived. Not only did he torture and murder his child victims but he would also cook and eat them. The icing on the cake however for the kinky little fourteen-year-old Dead Murderers Society girls was how grandaddy Fish would write letters to the dead children's grief-stricken parents informing them about just how tasty little Grace Budd and all the other missing children had been, documenting in lurid detail how he had fried their little livers and kidneys and served them with mashed potatoes and carrots. The Dead Murderers Society squealed with delight at this detail and, as usual, started getting into some serious teenage lesbo action, fanny licking, dildo-riding and fist-fucking before carrying on with the stories and gory details of the careers of the rest of their serial killer sexual heroes.

Because Brady wasn't dead he couldn't be mentioned at these junior lesbian pervert meetings. This didn't bother Tara too much as it meant that she had the handsome child killer all to herself. She had fond memories of her schooldays at Sherbourne, falling asleep masturbating lazily after reading the love letters the killer sent to her every day.

"Who cares about a few dead working class kids anyway, apart from the stupid tabloids?" she mumbled to herself as she drifted off into her beautiful dreams of blood and murder.

Tara bit the cotton with her teeth then stood back and admired her handiwork, both Peter and herself could hardly stop from laughing, so ridiculous did their little sex-change Dandelion look.

"I wonder if Mincey Harris is a switch hitter!" laughed Darklord.

"Darling, bisexuality is so passe these days. I'm sure he will be!" added cruel Tara, her mannish laughter ringing in poor

Dandelion's ears.

What had she done to deserve this!?

"Please!" the poor girl managed to croak through her toothless bleeding mouth. "Please. Just kill me, please..."

Dandelion passed out, Darklord and Tara never heard her. They were buggering away on the floor, orgasming like maniacs as they writhed in the gore that pooled at Dandy's broken feet.

Chapter Thirty Six

Frankie Auschwitz

Gerry Enchilada, The Leather Cowboys bear-like Mexican bass player, farted loudly on his latest bedfriend's leg. It was way after three in the afternoon and the sweaty lovers were still stinking in Gerry's pit. The young girl hit him on his back, she hated it when men farted in bed, let alone on her leg. She wasn't feeling too good, couldn't remember how she had even ended up in this fat snoring pig's tangled grey sheeted shagpit.

The sweet aroma of unwashed genitalia and arse crack grease curled around the room like diseased fog. She couldn't remember a thing. She opened her reddened eyes and groped for her cigarettes. Her arse was sore, the dirty bastard had obviously given her a serious seeing-to up the tradesmen's entrance. The floor of the derelict hellhole flat was a veritable polluted sea of empty tequila and beer bottles, ash trays overflowing with fags and roaches, horrible porno magazines with cunt-stretching whores drinking sperm and sucking the penises of horrible ugly men. She remembered downing hundreds of tequilla slammers with the bass player, Gerry whatsisname, in the Colepitz on Kilburn High Street, but the rest was a complete blank.

Poor little Fuckerada didn't even know if it was a school day or not. She hobbled to the bathroom to shit out loverboy's greasy spunk. Her arse was fucking killing her. She was hovering on the toilet trying to ease out a turd or two when she heard the phone ring. That dirty bastard, how had he managed to slide one up her shitter? She didn't even let her father do that.

Gerry felt as if the Luftwaffe had been using his head

for bomb practice. His hand shot out, knocking over a half empty tequila bottle as she picked up the phone. It was Strutter, he was in the phone box outside, he'd been banging on the door for half an hour. "Open the facking door, you chilli munching bastard!" or something like that.

The unshaven Mexican swung his legs over the bed, raised a cheek and let out a wet one.

"Shit!" he said, wiping the watery shit on the sheet and stumbled down the corridor scratching his greasy balls. "Wha's the focking emergency man..?" he grumbled, opening the door.

Strutter had a six pack of Tennents Super in his hand and was smiling like some kind of amphetamine believer.

"You ain't gonna facking believe this, man!" he shouted, slapping the bass player on his hairy naked arse.

"Hey, man, get off my ass, man, you turn focking homo or something?" snarled Gerry irritably. "You smile like you won the focking lottery, man!" he added, walking back into the bedroom and diving back into his disgusting pit.

"It's better than that, man!" said the grinning Strutter.

"What. man, what? You get laid or something?" shot the Latino.

"Frankie Auschwitz, man!" said Strutter, waiting for his friend's reaction.

"Frankie Auschwitz, what, man, what? You fock him or something?" Gerry was only half aware of the boss of the entire recording industry, some suit fucker with shitloads of money.

"Fucker only wants to sign us to his Cosmosodomistic record label."

"What you do, man? You suck his dick or something, man? Cos tha's the only way that cat would fockin' sign a bunch of fockin' bums like us, man!"

"No man, some big jeans company, man, they've been using 'Bumfucker Electric' on their latest advert! Frankie says if we re-release the track, man, it's gonna go straight to number one, he wants to meet up with us tonight to work out a deal man! Can you believe it!"

The fat Mexican sat up and scratched his balls.

"What about Mincey man? Does he know? Ain't no one seen him for like a month, man, ever since that Darklord cat stole his woman, man, he could be focking dead man, that would be more like our luck man, fockin' yeah!" The bass player coughed a resigned laugh, shaking his head wearily.

Strutter popped a couple of Supers and handed one to his friend, chugging hard on his own can of tramp's ruin.

"Drink your T man, we got to get straightened out, we're like meeting him in some fancy restaurant in a couple of hours!".

Gerry hadn't seen his guitarist buddy so happy since he copped off with some junkie supermodel chick in New York five years ago.

Strutter sprang up and headed to the bathroom.

"Hey Gerry, man!" he called from the disgusting lavatory, "I think you got a dead chick on your toilet, man, she looks pretty blue, man".

The Mexican ambled over to the shitty bog.

"No man, she jus' tired, we partied pretty hard las' night. Jus' put her on the floor, man, she'll be alright, she jus' sleeping, she ain't fockin' blue , man, you gotta stop scarin' me like that, man, i's not funny man, fockin' asshole, wa's wrong with you?"

****

Frankie Auschwitz snapped off a wad of zoophiliac spunk up his beloved Irish setter's dog cunt and fell back onto his silk sheets, the docile bitch wagged her tail and started licking her owner's face. Frankie whispered loving baby talk into the silky animal's ear, pursing his lips. allowing his adored pet to lick the fleshy protuberances.

"Oh daddy's baby, yes you are, mmm, yes, yes yes!"

Frankie loved his Irish setters, he had two of them - Babykins Apple Pie and Pixie Trixabelle.

Why couldn't human beings be more like dogs? Undemanding, loyal and loving. Even when they were kicked half to death by a drunken master they would still humbly lick the hand that battered them.

Frankie luxuriated in his huge marble and gold sunken bath, listening to the soothing sounds of George Michael and Simply Red. Ah yes, George and Mick, the zoophilliac's favourite singers! In some strange way they reminded him of his beloved Irish Setters.

Not like those wild mongrels, The Leather Cowboys. Twenty years ago he had wanted to sign those boys up - they were wild, untamed, sexy! If only it weren't for that unfortunate incident with his troubled son and Strutter. Oh well, the boy was dead now and a businessman shouldn't bear grudges if they got in the way of an opportunity for making a few easy millions - small change for a man of his wealth admittedly, but, as his old mother used to say, pennies and pounds, something about them looking after themselves. Or something.

He eventually heaved himself out of the bath, he was in surprisingly good condition for a man of 61, he was lean, a little stooped maybe, but when he wore his toupee he looked at least ten years younger.

Babykins Apple Pie ran up to her master and started licking his balls.

"My goodness, Babykins, not again, we made love at least four times last night..."

He laughed pushing the beloved animal away..The record company uberboss took a stroll on the veranda of his huge penthouse. It had one of the best views in London. High on the Northern side of the Thames, it commanded a glorious sweep of nearly all the capital's most famous landmarks as well as a magnificent stretch of that mysterious waterway, the Thames. The Houses of Parliament, Nelson's column, St Pauls Cathedral, Battersea power station, all were in plain view from his superb luxury apartment.

Frankie considered himself a cultured man and had a

well stocked library consisting almost exclusively the best sellers over the past forty years. Jeffery Archer was his favourite author. Jeff was a man who understood the vagaries and intimacies of power and money well. Power and money were - after all - the only things that really mattered at the end of the day.

Frankie was a proud man. The riches and influence he had achieved, he achieved himself. No influential parents or noble birth had got him where he was today. He was one of those striving, driven creatures; a self made man.

Born in Liverpool to lower middle class parents, his father had been headmaster of an unremarkable grammar school. Frankie had first tasted success as keyboard player in a local psychedelic band The Arsehole Implodes. Unfortunately, within the tight constraints and rigid energies that make up a band there's seldom room for two over-inflated egos, Frankie had already started losing his hair in his late teens, so he made the decision to stand down. After all he was sharp enough to realise that the cats on the other side of the desks held the power, which was Frankie's real desire, beautiful power and beautiful money.

He decided to start his own label with money he had managed to swindle from his frail grandmother, she was going to die soon anyway and she couldn't take it with her, reasoned the shrewd business mogul.

He took a series of motivation courses which stressed the need for having no conscience whatsoever if one was to flourish and survive the cutthroat world of business. And so he had developed an almost spiritual philosophy of complete and utter Ultra Bastardism..

With the money he had swindled out of Grandma he set up his own record label - SHIT Records. The logo had a picture of a pigeon eating a lump of crap. Over the next 20 years the driven young man ascended the greasy pole of the music business faster than a paedophile let loose in Disneyland. The wealth he acquired. however, made him prey to every gold digging bitch in the world. Rather than risk losing any of his billions to some peroxide slut he decided that any sexual intimacies he required from now on would come only from his beautiful dogs. Frankie often remembers his first love - a beautiful, haughty Afghan hound called Princess Lucretia who, after all these years, still has a place in his heart. He spent over two million pounds in bribes having her buried in St Pauls.

The service was beautiful, he cried for days.

Chapter Thirty Seven

Mellow twisted, big time.

By the time the stretch limo called round for Strutter and Gerry, both Leather Cowboys were fucked. They'd finished off the six pack of Tennants Super, smoked a shit load of skunk to get them mellow, got a little too mellow, so cracked open a bottle of Tequila and did some shots using methedrine instead of salt to unmellow themselves.

"I think my mellow's twisted, man," said Gerry from the toilet, he was squeezing out last night's two donor kebabs and noticed that the girl was still asleep on the floor, she did look a little blue he thought and then put it out of his mind. Even some OD'd schoolkid wasn't going to ruin this buzz. The fat beaner pulled up his bootcut jeans and pulled down the waistband at the back so you could just make out his brickie's cleavage, he knew chicks really dug that.

"Man, when we get some money man, I'm going down to Acapulco man, gonna go fockin' loco down in Acupulco,. man! Fockin' chix down there man you ain't seen nothin' like it, man, loco man, loco in Acapulco, yeah" The methedrine had kicked in but the tequila and beer and skunk had kind of got them sort of sideways mellow again, kind of. But they were working fast, like in the mind, so if this Frankie Auschwitz guy tried to rip them off, their super intellectual minds would know straight away. They did a gramme of coke each in the back of the limo just to make them extra intelligent so they wouldn't get ripped off.

"Yeah, man, we see right through that cat if he tries to rip us off, man, yeah," said Gerry opening another wrap and hoovering a huge pile off the end of his switch blade.

"Here, Strutter, man, have the last of this" said the major intellectual power of the 21st century, offering a huge white mountain from the end of his knife to Strutter. "We can't be smart enough man, this cat, Auschwitz, he's clever, man, finish off that coke, man. I got a couple of rocks we can smoke jus' before we go in, yeah man, intelligent man, don' let him rip us off, man, no way, man., we gotta be smart, man…Know what I'm sayin'?"

This was typical Cowboys behaviour, even without Mincey around the two chumps were blowing the deal before they even got to the meeting. The two outer-spacers had gone from mellow, through twisted mellow, to sideways mellow and into total paranoia in just under ten minutes without even realising.

"I need some smack, man.." said Gerry as they rolled up to the exclusive Welsh restaurant in Mayfair. Strutter had piped up his rock and was handing Gerry the coke tin and lighter, the Mexican took a hit on his crack and felt better immediately. For about a minute.

The Maitre d' showed them to their table, this was the snazziest joint either of them had ever seen. Welsh cuisine was the height of fashion, Gerry figured this out because there were no prices on the small menu.

The comedown from the crack was kicking in badly, he felt depressed, like lead.

"Man, I'm gonna have to do this smack in the toilet man, you got any foil man?" Gerry called over a waiter. "Hey man, do you like sell Kit Kats or anything man?"

The waiter raised a supercilious eyebrow.

"Would sir like to see the desert menu?"

"Fock no man, I need a Kit Kat or something, with silver paper man, fock."

"Oh, I see, one moment sir" said the waiter. He returned from the kitchen with a large piece of kitchen foil and a book of matches. "The washrooms are over there, sir," he said, placing the tray on the immaculate white tablecloth

"Thanks, man!" said Gerry hurrying to the washroom. Strutter waited a moment, his hands were shaking real bad. Then the guitarist got to his feet unsteadily and followed his buddy into the toilet.

The brown brought them down fast, like some kind of pharmaceutical elevator.

Like a couple of icebergs they drifted back to their table, ready to do business with Frankie Dogfucker.

Unfortunately the first thing the megaboss of the entire recording industry did when he arrived was chop out six fat lines of primo Columbian on a silver tray, right there on the table, even asking the waiter for three straws.

No musician, like, not even the squeakiest clean cut kiddie popper. can turn down free drugs. Within seconds of snorting the cocaine their paranoia returned like some fucked up ugly boomerang they couldn't get rid of.

"No way man! Tha's like the oldest trick in the book man! Fockin' blank check man! Whaddayou think were like fockin' idiots man! We write our own check man! As much money as we want! What you think we're idiots man! Fock you man!" said sharp Gerry Enchilada, shrewd business man of the year

"Yeah man!" joined in Strutter. "Do we look facking stupid or something! We can have as much money as we want?! You facking suits man! All the facking same! Complete artistic control, ten mill up front!? Fack you, man! Don't piss down my back, man, and tell me it's raining!" shouted Strutter.

"Yeah man!" added Gerry, as confused as Frankie by Strutter's last proclamation. "And don't shit in my cowboy boots either, man, and say its fockin' snowing!" he added with slightly less conviction, following Strutter out of the door, grabbing a couple of bread rolls for later.

Frankie Auschwitz, in all his years as the international king of everything in the music business, had never seen anything like it. Here he was with a blank cheque, offering these loser bums as much money as they wanted and complete and utter artistic control and they'd told him to go and fuck himself, taken his bag of cocaine and stormed out of the best Welsh restaurant in London before the hors d'ouevres had even arrived.

He had to sign them.

Period.

Chapter Thirty Eight

Brownsabre Security

Amos Arsebottom and Bob Sockett took it in turns on the gates of the Darklord weirdo's stately castle home. The pair of them should have been on full alert but the gaffer of their security firm BROWNSABRE SECURITY never bothered checking on them.

The security of the rock star's home was considered an easy earner. The only way into the place was up the winding road and through the gates. The house backed onto one of the steepest cliffs in the whole range of the Bingley mountains and was surrounded by forty foot walls with CCTV on every turret. An extra 6 foot of electrified razor wire sat on top of the walls, making them virtually unassailable. Even if any supersonic burglar made it up the 40 mile twisting road and over the wall, there were fifty ex SAS and ex-Executive Outcome security guards armed to the teeth with Uzi sub-machine guns, powerful Colt Commando assault rifles, stun guns, pepper spray, electric tazers and the biggest, most vicious looking Bull Mastiffs this side of the middle ages. No wonder Amos and Bob took it easy, the place was fucking impregnable.

But then again Amos and Bob had never met the Aztecs of Sodom.

The last thing Amos Arsebottom saw as he lit his Macho Light cigarette was the huge barechested biker giant Rapeman Rape, smiling in the sodium spotlight outside the heavy steel gates, a huge fucking anti-tank gun balanced on his shoulder.

As he fired the armour piercing shell, the headlights of forty Harley Davidson 74's switched on as one. The shell boomed from the barrel, trailing fire and smashing into the gates, vapourising both them and the body of Amos Arsebottom into a bloody haze. The dozy Brownsabre guards stopped masturbating, smoking, reading and drinking and reached for their weapons as The Aztecs of Sodom roared through the burning gates like demons from hell.

The Brownsabre men sprayed round after round at the terrifying Aztecs yet not one of them fell. In fact the terrified corporate cocksucking fuckers killed several of their own number in the crossfire. The Aztecs swept through the useless guard like death itself. Many of the Brownsabre guards hadn't seen action for over 20 years and were sliced to ribbons by the Aztecs' hatchets, cutlasses, bowie-knives, nail-studded baseball bats, machetes and diamond-studded knuckledusters. The Aztecs grabbed the semi-automatics from the fallen guards and started carving the whole screaming bunch into bloody confetti using highly accurate bursts of rapid fire. The whole courtyard was aflame with death and destruction, goresplattered bodies flying around like scarlet rag dolls, the mastiffs too, man and dog indistinguishable in the cyclone of gore.

The Aztecs had started efficiently sodomising their victims as well. The still living guards, the ones who had run out of bullets or had tried to flee into the castle, were having their ringpieces buggered all to bloody hell. Rapeman Rape and Horsecock Satan had one poor bastard on the spit, the wretched cunt's screams choking on Horsecock's awesome 20-inch spamjagger, drowning on a cocktail of sperm and his own blood. Jesus Con Carne was spraying the courtyard with two Uzi's, laughing insanely and cursing in Spanish. The whole place was like some hellish ballet, bodies flying this way and that, somersaulting around and around as the bullets turned them into tattered offal. Blood, gallons and gallons of the stuff splashed around the stone floor as the bikers waded into the dead and dying, laughing like madmen, mopping up with huge hunting knives, slashing throats and stamping on heads with their heavy jackboots. Fountains of arterial blood, huge arcs rose out of the hamburger slop, covering the bikers from head to toe making them look like grinning, white toothed, scarlet dripping Hellions.

Brown magician Bill Drummond, naked but covered in a protective suit of his own shite, was running around screaming, hacking into the dying guards with a hatchet, ripping off heads and throwing them towards the guards cowering at the locked heavy door of the castle. The demented Scot was lost in the white hot passion of battle and had started to emulate the Aztecs, violently buggering any bloody arsehole he could find, bucking away into headless, armless torsos, fucking the bleeding mouths of the severed heads.

The gunfire ceased as quickly as it had started, The Aztecs stopping firing as one - so in tune with each other were their battle skills. The smoke cleared on a scene of utter and total carnage, it was impossible to tell where one mess of intestines, splintered bone and meat ended and the other one started. It just seemed to be a huge pile of guts, intestines, bones and gore. Bill hadn't even noticed that the battle had been won, so intense was his gut thrashing buggery. He was banging away in a naked guard's fucked-up arse, chewing on the face of a severed head, sucking out the eyeballs and swallowing them down with the blood pumping from the neck of another head. Not one Aztec had fallen. Their wars in the African theatre had made them almost completely invincible. Horsecock Satan had taken a single bullet through his side, but was already sewing up the wound himself.

Poor Mincey had taken shelter in the shattered guardroom by the twisted metal gates, crouching down amongst the broken glass and gore, the poor musician was trembling uncontrollably, a nervous wreck. He'd never seen anything like it, not even on TV. He was on the verge of spasming into a nervous fit when his old friend Zodiac, who remained as immaculate as ever, not a drop of blood anywhere on the man, handed him some kind of glass phial. It was from the guardroom's first aid supplies, pure unadulterated intramuscular heroin.

"Stick the needle into your thigh and snap the end off the glass," said the cool hero, Mincey was instinctive when it came to gear and did as he was told without hesitation, the rush hit him almost immediately, that warm locomotive flattening of reality sliding him into a cool warm mellow, he didn't even flinch when one of Z's silver throwing knives whizzed past his face and pinned the last remaining guard to the wall.

Down in the bowels of the castle, beneath a secret network of tunnels cut deep into the black rock of the Bingley mountains, Peter Darklord and his perverted lover shivered in fear. They'd watched the whole battle on CCTV. Not even the servants knew about this secret room or the booby trapped tunnels that led from the master bedroom down to this impregnable inner sanctum. There was enough food and champagne to last them a year if necessary. Peter had had all the workers and the architect who designed the tunnels and the room secretly assasinated. Sometimes it paid to be paranoid thought the terrified Darklord.

"Why didn't we bring the girl!" shrieked Tara, she was just this side of total screaming hysteria and was getting increasingly on Peter's already frayed tits.

"Is that all you can think about at a time like this!" screamed the terrified Darklord. "Fucking nooky!? Did you see what those fucking bastards did to my men!? Brownsabre security are one of the most ruthlessly efficient organisation of security gorillas in the country and those fucking bikers shot them and buggered them into dogmeat within minutes! You're fucking mad woman! Fucking MAAAD!!!!!"

The gothic frontman lashed out and punched Tara full in the face. Cutting his knuckle on her teeth, he pulled back his hand, part of one of Tara's front teeth was stuck in his bloody knuckle.

"Now look what you've done, you mental fucking bitch!" He kicked her hard in the cunt. Tara screamed and leapt at him, trying to take out his eyes with her nails.

"You fucking idiot!" she screamed, raking a bloody chunk out of his face. "I wasn't thinking of using her for torture fun, I was thinking of using her as a hostage! What if they find us down here!"

Darklord looked worried.

"Impossible! No one knows about this place except us, none of the servants, no one!" he said angrily, but his tone of voice belied the confidence of his words. Darklord had thought his castle impregnable but it had taken a gang of sodomistic bikers and three weirdo rockers only twenty minutes to destroy the castle gates and obliterate his entire security force. He banged the controls on the CCTV to check the inside of the castle door. The bikers, Mindwarp and Harris were already in the hallway. A weird naked guy covered in shit was staring straight at the camera and smiling horribly, he was doing some kind of little farting dance and wanking himself off.

"That guy's fucking sick!" said Tara, wrinkling her surgically perfect nose and pointing at the brown magician on the screen.

Chapter Thirty Nine

Sledgehammers, Machine Guns and
Cold, Cold Beds.

Mindwarp ordered the men to sweep the castle and bring anyone they found down to the hallway. He lit a Camel Light and offered one to the gouching Mince.

"She's facking dead, man, isn't she?" said Mincey, flat, as if he didn't care. Zodiac knew that was the heroin, he knew Mincey did care. Dandelion had been the singer's light at the end of the shitty, rat infested sewer that was his excuse for a life, his only hope of salvation.

Although Mindwarp was intellectually and emotionally beyond the simplistic constructs of love and hate, he recognized that these two powerful illusions were the very bedrock of western civilisation.

Without the legacy bequeathed to the western soul by those primal orchard thieves, all that would be left would be that terrible, infinite abyss that lurks at the centre of everything. That luminescent darkness of despair and pointlessness that had tumbled over-sophisticated civilisations into decadence and extinction within a single generation.

It was the Ubermen, those metaphysical athletes and serious poets, men like Zodiac Mindwarp, who had to wrestle with these scary monsters, for all of our sakes. Brave philosophers with sledgehammers and machineguns.

Sledgehammers, machineguns and cold, cold beds.

For Mincey, however, and rightly so, love was all.

And there was a deep and yearning part of the existential philosopher Rock God superhero Zodiac Mindwarp, that envied him this warm and comforting illusion.

"She's alive, Mincey, I know it," he said patting the doped degenerate on his bony shoulders, not really giving a fuck either way, but pretending he did, for some weird reason or another.

Mincey started to cry, huge wracking sobs, Z handed him another phial of emergency smack, he hated seeing grown men cry..

Horsecock Satan and Rapeman Rape threw Darklord's servants down the grand oak staircase and followed behind them laughing.

"They say they don't know where their master is!" said Rapeman, kicking an elderly grandfather in the bollocks. "I don't believe them boss," he said, punching an old woman in the face, her false teeth shattering and flying across the hallway. "Come on you old bitch!" He shouted in the grandmother's terrified face, she was crying, protesting her innocence. Horsecock Satan had unzipped his terrifying trousersnake and was waving it at the frail white haired old lady.

"Please" she managed to say through her bleeding mouth "I have no idea...". She was crying and obviously telling the truth. "I haven't seen the master for over a week, I'm just the cook. In the name of God...."

"She's telling the truth, you idiots," said Zodiac, stepping up and shooting her in the face, her neck snapping backwards, her toothless face exploding in a shower of blood, shattered bone and brains.

"What about you, grandad?" said Z, sticking his fine Heckler&Koch machine-pistol in the quaking butler's mouth. The man tried to speak, his mouth forming the words but his abject terror preventing any sound escaping from his doomed lips. The impatient Sex God blasted another head from its shoulders, a huge fountain of blood gushing from the neck and splattering over the blonde chambermaids. Five of them. Sexy little cunts, tits and everything. Bang!Bang!Bang!Bang!Bang!

They didn't know either.

It was Jesus Con Carne who found Dandy, he didn't

know who she was but figured she must the Mincer's chick.

"She's over in the tower, she's pretty fucked up man" said the vice president to Zodiac "To be honest I think she's dead" he added, eyeing the pathetic sight of the Mincer.

Mincey was so whacked on the powerful hospital gear, he just stared blankly. He heard what the biker said, knew what he was supposed to feel, but was insulated within the emotional flatland of his 20-year-old habit.

"You want to check it out man?" said Z, "'It could be someone else."

The Mincer shrugged and they followed the humongo biker up the stairs, stepping over the spreading pool of blood leaking from the five wasted blondes. Bill lingered furtively, eyes narrowed, a truly creepy expression on his face, and fingered one of the dead young women, hooking deep with his middle digit and and pulling hard, he grabbed himself a handful of dead tit and cranked off a twelve second turkey murder, jizzing a fat shiny oyster across what was left of the corpse's splattered features.

The excromancer caught up with Mincey, Z and Jesus. The borderline necro didn't want to miss this little find, even the battlehardened Con Carne seemed slightly perturbed at what he'd come across. The excromancer discerned a slight ripple of excitement in his brown underpants and it was only seconds ago that he'd jammed off on the pretty chambermaid.

"In there, man!" said Jesus nervously, and this a man who had endured and contributed to the most savage, horrific, theatre of war in the world, the disembowelled bloodstain of equatorial Africa. "I'll wait out here if you don't mind"

Bill puked first, quickly followed by poor Mincey, even the smack couldn't blot out the emotional intensity that seared through his soul, what had they done to his Dandy? Why had they done this to his Dandy. "In the name of God..." he exhaled..

He'd prayed on the long walk down the dark corridor that it was some other poor bitch in this flyblown room. The stench was making his eyes water, there were flies in their thousands, buzzing around the the rancid miasma, the stench, like dead dog curry shit, rotten meat, corruption - the poor bastard hurled again. For a split second his heart had lifted when he saw the dripping thing hanging from the St Andrews cross - it had a cock. But there was no mistaking those huge tits, even covered in dried black blood and minus nipples they were obviously Dandy's big fucking mashers. Her beautiful black hair, her swollen, battered face covered in blood, her eyes, just two slits. She hung there still, dead. Mincey, tears running down his face and mingling with vomit, wandered up to the body of his love. Those sick, sick bastards! A severed penis was stitched onto the remains of his love's sewn up, suppurating cunt.

"Clam, clamjungle.." the destroyed singer half sang, cried, he grabbed hold of the filthy, diseased cock and ripped it off, stamping it beneath his feet. He walked around the back, the nipples sewn onto her beautiful young buttocks, oh my god! What had they done to her arsehole!? Mincey fell to his knees, just a gaping black hole, flies eating the blood, shit and pus running down the back of her legs, oh God oh god oh god...

"If there is a God??!" shouted Mincey at the ceiling, balling his fists dramatically and shaking them at the heavens. "Then I curse you! Fack you God! You pig! Bastard! Bastard! I'll side with the Devil! Damn YOU! DAMN FACK SHIT YOU!" screamed the devastated singer.

"Mincey!" It was Z, he was untying the girl's wrists hastily. "She's alive! Quick man!"

Mincey sprang to his feet, pulling at the leather bonds. Jesus entered the room and slashed the ropes with his huge Bowie knife. Z had his head on the girl's chest, he started banging hard, Dandy started coughing, blood and bile in huge gouts. Mincey sat her up and started hitting her face.

"Dandy, baby, can you hear me!? It's Mincey! Oh please God, I take it all back, I take it all back, Clamjungle, Clamjungle !Oh baby, baby talk to me" pleaded her lover, Dandy's toothless mouth opened slightly.

"M.i..n..c..y...." she breathed, barely audible, she belched a huge wad of blood onto the singers face and winced in agony as he embraced her.

Bill had already taken a magical shit and was preparing a poultice from his mystic bab. The girl lifted her arm weakly and pointed at the wall.

"In...there" she hissed weakly.

"In..the.. wall..Darklor...His woma..n" she gasped before passing out from loss of blood.

Down in the basement, the vile Darklord and his whore looked at each other in terror. Their pale sick features blue from the light of the CCTV monitor, their bowels turned to water, they knew the game was up.

Chapter Forty

Bumfucker Electric

The vertigo horns of Wagner's 'Ride of the Valkyries' were teetering at the peak of their atmospheric weirdness when Gerry Enchilados growling bass intro scootered out of the dry ice, Robbie's scattergun drumroll propelled the Leather Cowboys into the riffmonster beast of 'Bumfucker Electric', their first number one.

Mincey ran from the wings, pyros exploding all over the place, tongue flickering like a fast-forward rattler hunting down gashdogs in the Arizona desert.

He grabbed the mike, cockstrutting insanely, hands on hips, snapping back and forth from the hips like a double jointed Steven Tyler, the bendy Aerosmith frontman.

The capacity crowd at Hammersmith Odeon went berserk.

"Bumfucker! Bumfucker! Bumfucker Baby! You're Electric! alright!" bawled the Mincer. "I got the cock! And you got the socket, baby! Alright!"

Mincey had been at Dandy's side in the Bingley infirmary intensive care ward when he got the phonecall from Gerry telling him that Frankie Auschwitz wanted to sign the band for a ridiculous ninety million quid advance worldwide.

Revenge is a dish best served cold - or so the saying goes.

Not in Mincey Harris's book. For the Mincer, who despite all his flaws was a noble man, revenge was a dish best not served at all.

For all he knew, Peter Darklord and his sick whore were still hiding in the stupid dungeon of his stupid castle. No one he reasoned, could hurt those fuckers more than they could hurt each other.

Two million quid and the best plastic surgeon in Rio De Janeiro had patched Dandy up as good as new, even her arsehole.

His love danced madly down the front as the band crashed into 'Clamjungle Pie'. The loving couple had got married at Gracelands in the spring.

The Cowboys' last album had gone triple platinum in the States, the world had been waiting for some down and dirty Cowboy rock for years and here it was at last, courtesy of Cosmosodomistic records and that dirty old dog lover Frankie Auschwitz.

Zodiac, Bill and the Aztecs drank their Tennents Super at the bar, laughing hard as the band kicked into the Leather Cowboys classic 'Blow job Queen!'.

"BLOW JOB QUEEN, YOU KNOW WHAT I MEAN! SHE'S OUTRAAAAGEOUSSS!!" bawled Mincey and Strutter on the same mike.

"BLOW JOB QUEEN!YES SHE IS, ALRIGHT HAMMERSMIIITHH! WOOH! YEAHH!"

Cosmic space age boogie baby, Yeah!

The End

ALSO AVAILABLE FROM ATTACK!
VATICAN BLOODBATH

The 500 year long struggle between the Vatican and the British Royal Family for control of the world's drug trade is about to reach a thrilling and unutterably bloody climax...

This is the thriller to end all thrillers - a brutal bastard of a two-fisted ripping yarn that makes Frederick Forsyth read like the Teletubbies on tamazipan!

by Tommmy Udo

ALSO AVAILABLE FROM ATTACK!

WHIPS & FURS

MY LIFE AS A GAMBLER, BON VIVANT AND LOVE RAT

BY

JESUS H. CHRIST

EDITED AND INTRODUCED BY STEWART HOME

ALSO AVAILABLE FROM ATTACK!
TITS-OUT TEENAGE TERROR TOTTY

"OBTAIN PERMISSION FROM WHOEVER PAYS YOUR PSYCHIATRIC HOSPITAL BILLS BEFORE READING THIS BOOK."
THE FACE

"AWESOME BOOK! This is the BEST reading I ever had!! Everyone should order a copy of this brilliant book today! Nobody writes like Steven Wells does! You will not be disappointed!" (5 stars) AMAZON.COM

by Steven Wells

ALSO AVAILABLE FROM ATTACK!

SATAN! SATAN! SATAN!

THE MINDBLOWING EXPOSE OF BRITAIN'S SEX-CRAZY SATANIC ROCK'N'ROLL KIDS

From the legendary creator of the crustie-cult classic 'Road Rage' comes a story so disturbing that the author has had to go into hiding!

by Tony White

ALSO AVAILABLE FROM ATTACK!
RAIDERS OF THE LOW FOREHEAD

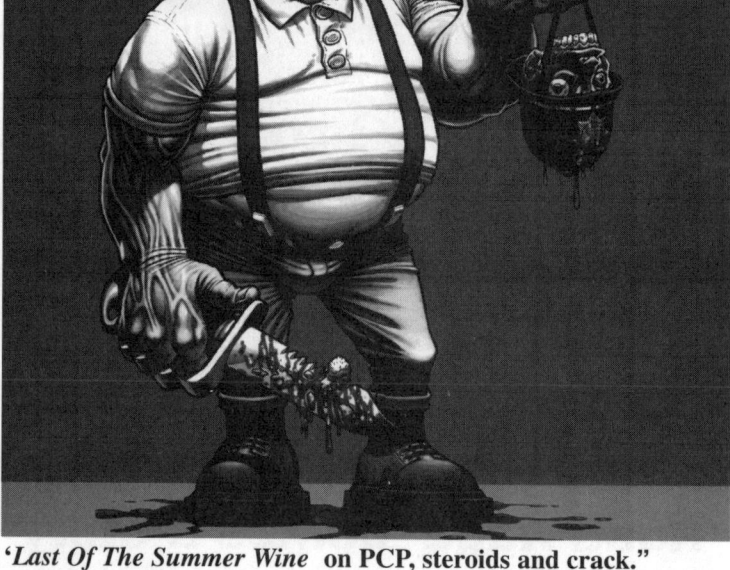

'*Last Of The Summer Wine* on PCP, steroids and crack."
The Big Issue
"Sicker than an outbreak of Ebola in an Orphanage."
The List
'I found *Raiders* hilarious! It's fast, crass, sick and demented. Reading it is like being tied to a roller coaster."
Pennie Hoffman

by Stanley Manly